ALL THE WHILE

THE COLLEGE PACT SERIES

GINA AZZI

All the While

Copyright © 2019 by Gina Azzi

THE COLLEGE PACT SERIES

Four best friends.
Four sexy athletes.
Four hot romances.
One college pact!

The Last First Game (Lila's Story)
All the While (Maura's Story)
Me + You (Emma's Story)
Kiss Me Goodnight in Rome (Mia's Story)

AUGUST

1

MAURA

I wasn't always promiscuous.

In fact, I never slept around until my twin, Adrian, disappeared from my life.

Before that, I cared too much about upholding the values our parents raised us with to ever have a slew of one-night stands. But when he stopped playing by the rules, I figured why shouldn't I?

And that's how it started.

The drinking, the sex, the painful loneliness that eats pieces of my heart and gnaws at my soul. Even when I'm surrounded by my rowing team or hanging with my best friends, Emma, Lila, and Mia, I'm so alone it hurts to breathe in too deep.

Like if I do, I'll shatter the façade I'm trying so hard to keep up.

So, I drink.

Wine. Vodka. Tequila.

Anything to numb my body from absorbing the shock of Adrian's loss.

Anything to numb my mind from processing that he's gone, from addressing the anger I'm harboring over his death.

Because the truth is, I'm furious at my twin for leaving me behind.

But how can you stay angry at a dead person when the rest of his world placed him on a pedestal?

My mom can't mention his name without tears welling in the corners of her eyes. My dad prefers to pretend that everything is fine.

And so I'm utterly alone.

Alone in my thoughts, alone in my grief, and definitely alone in my anger which, some days, threatens to consume me.

To embrace the numbing detachment I've come to rely on, I need to drink.

I need to inhale the calming sweetness of Marlboro Menthol Golds like no athlete before me ever has.

I need to have lots of deliciously mind-numbing sex with random men.

In the mornings that follow, I wash their scent off of my skin and pretend the night before never happened. And if I'm really lucky, I can hardly remember the night at all.

The only thing I don't touch, never have, never will, is drugs.

Because as much as I miss my brother, I'm furious with him for taking his own life. Sure, he didn't intend to at the time. But isn't an overdose just as selfish as suicide?

I keep my head down and my grades up. I attend rowing practices on time, dig into each and every catch, my hair tucked into one of Adrian's old baseball caps, my sunglasses hiding the void in my eyes. And even though everyone knows something is wrong, something is off, no one can figure out what it is.

Until Zack, Adrian's best friend, intervenes.

I just don't know it yet.

———

"ARE YOU AWAKE?" Mia's whisper cuts through the silence of her childhood bedroom. She's sitting up, her elbow propped against the pillows resting in front of her headboard.

"Who?" Lila asks sleepily.

"Any of you?" Mia whispers.

"Why are you whispering? We're all obviously awake." Emma's voice booms. She sits up in bed next to Mia. I can just make out her shadowy silhouette from my spot on the air mattress at the foot of the bed. "Right, Maura?"

"I am now," I answer.

"Do you think it's a good idea?" Mia asks.

"What?" Lila sits up next to me. The mattress dips dangerously low on my side as she shifts her weight. She runs her fingers through her golden waves lazily. "Is what a good idea?"

"Going to Rome?" Mia's voice is still a whisper.

"Yes!" We all exclaim in unison. Lila flops back down next to me and the air mattress lurches under my shoulder blades.

"It's going to be great, Mia, you'll see," Emma says reassuringly. "This semester, it's going to be epic. We're all going on such exciting adventures!" Her voice is alive with the anticipation of the future, of the unknown. An awkward silence settles as my best friends acknowledge that I'm not going on an adventure.

I'm not going anywhere.

"And you're going to win Dad Vail this year!" Emma tries, overcompensating with her enthusiasm.

"Yeah, it will be great."

"Seriously, Maura," Lila picks up where Emma leaves off, "the pact ... it's about pushing past our comfort zones, erasing some of those boundaries that have been restricting us. It's about having fun and letting go, for one semester. You can do that from anywhere." Her voice holds a note of a challenge that irritates me.

Stupid college pact. We all agreed earlier today, while eating pizza and drinking sangria at one of Mia's favorite New York restaurants, that we would live it up this semester. Be wild, be courageous, be brave, try new things, blah, blah, blah. And it makes sense. It really does ... if you're Mia, Emma, or Lila.

They're going on real adventures, leaving McShain University behind. They're starting new chapters with new people in new places. Tomorrow morning Mia flies to Rome, Italy to study abroad. Emma is heading to Washington, D.C. for an internship on Capitol Hill. And Lila, who keeps joking about the killer tan she's going to sport and the hot guys she's going to meet, is participating in a medical internship through Astor University in California. They're all going on adventures, already pushing past their comfort zones, moving the invisible lines that demarcate their self-imposed boundaries.

But I'm not.

Nope. Not me.

I'm heading back to our campus at McShain University, still in Philadelphia, back to rowing. I'm not being wild, or courageous, or brave. Unless you count hitting up my old neighborhood to slum it with some of the guys, like Hector, who I know still kick it there.

Sighing heavily, I turn so Lila won't detect the tears brimming in my eyes. I'm going to be lost without these girls. Even at my worst, things seem manageable when they're around to keep me in check. But now, with all of them gone and wrapped up in the excitement of their new lives, I really will be on my own. Completely alone.

"Sure," I say into the silence, trying to sound confident.

No one buys it.

Mia turns on her reading lamp and the light bathes half her face in a warm glow. "Trust me, Maura, if I can get on a plane to Rome tomorrow morning, you can have an incredible semester and an even better start to the season."

"I know."

Because this is what I always wanted, isn't it?

This year, this season, is the culmination of everything I've worked for: endless hours of practice in the freezing rain, summer camps, two-a-days, torn hands coated with blisters the size of grapes, stress fractures layering my ribs. All of it was for this season so McShain University's women's rowing would be the best, number one, team in the United States.

It's what we always dreamed about. Adrian and me. He rowed for LaFarge University, also in Philadelphia. Being near him is one of the reasons I chose to attend McShain. That, and the full-ride scholarship. Still, being close to Adrian was an important determining factor. I mean, we're twins; we've practically been joined at the hip since before we were born. It's funny, really, people always think twins have some sort of special connection or bond. I never thought about it before or gave the idea much merit. Except now that he's gone, it's as if half of me is missing. We spent our whole lives growing together, and I don't want to move forward on my own. Alone.

Now that he's gone, I don't know how to keep holding on to half a dream.

Moments of silence tick by, and I hear Emma's soft snore. Lila snorts next to me, and Mia chuckles. Keeping my eyes closed, I feign sleep as they continue to talk about their semesters in new places.

Listening to their chatter, nerves spike in my bloodstream.

When did we grow into adults?

When did everything change?

Any why am I always being left behind?

2

ZACK

I'm unsettled.

In fact, as the wheels of the plane touch down at Philadelphia International Airport, I feel like a freshman, a novice, all over again.

For three years, Adrian Rodriguez was my best friend, my roommate, and sat in front of me, the sixth seat in our Varsity Eight.

In May, I fucking killed him.

Not by putting a gun to his head and pulling the trigger or running him over with my car. No, what I did was much worse. I missed the signs. I overlooked his mood swings and made excuses for his lying. I let him drift farther and farther away from me that by the time I called him out on his drug habit, I barely recognized the guy standing in front of me.

What type of best friend, roommate, teammate does that?

Now I'm back for senior year and I'm dreading it. None of it, not the academics, or the future plan to score a sick job in New York City, or my final rowing season makes any sense without Adrian.

Each morning brings a fresh wave of guilt, so overwhelming, I wonder when I'll finally drown in it.

I pray to drown in it.

Exiting the airport, I hail a cab to campus. The city air feels nothing like a homecoming. The usual excitement that zings with the start of the school year is gone. The thought of catching up with my rowing team after summer break feels obligatory. Too much of an emotional vortex for one day.

Rowing is no longer an outlet but a curse.

And as much as a part of me wants to quit, I can't.

Because I have unfinished business with the sport and with Adrian.

I need our boat to win the Dad Vail Regatta. For him.

STEPPING INTO MY HOUSE, a torrent of memories assaults me.

Adrian tossing an Xbox controller at D'Arco's head.

The guys all eating pizza, cracking up at Adrian's impersonations.

Adrian swearing at the television during a soccer match.

Adrian. Adrian. Adrian.

Shaking my head, I carry my bag up to my room, close my bedroom door, and drop my forehead against the wall, steadying my breath and squashing the swell of emotion that clogs my chest.

I share the house with three other guys from the crew team. It used to be five of us; now we're four. Damien D'Arco, Jeremy Hunt, James Bilson, and me. No one mentioned getting a new house for senior year, so we all just kept this one, closing Adrian's room off as if it doesn't even exist. And in a way, it doesn't, not without him to breathe life into it.

How the hell am I supposed to do this? Live here? Row? Graduate?

The house is quiet as I pull out my laptop and collapse onto my bed. The rest of the guys will be arriving sometime today since we start practice tomorrow morning. The only silver lining in keeping this house from last year is that none of us need to unpack and set up the space again. We all left it exactly the way it was on the last day we were all here.

Dad Vail Regatta.

Settling back against my pillows, I sign into my laptop, ignore the messages from my sister Nicole, click out of the emails regarding pre-class assignments, and log into Facebook.

My breath catches in my throat, a stab in my chest.

Because the first photo on my feed is Maura.

Maura Rodriguez.

Adrian's twin sister.

Staring at her face in the photo hurts.

She looks so similar to Adrian; the shape of their eyes, the determination glaring from them, is exact. She's smiling in a photo with her three best friends and while her friends' faces glow, there's something sinister about Maura's smirk.

Glancing at the caption posted by Emma Stanton, my jaw tightens until it aches.

Caption: On to new adventures, new beginnings, and an epic start to senior year! #collegepact.

Except Maura doesn't look excited for her fresh start; she looks devastated.

She's grieving, hell, we all are, but the pain bleeding from her midnight eyes alludes to something darker than sorrow, deeper than mourning.

A ball of shame burns in my stomach because I did this; I put that look in Maura's eyes, broke her fucking heart, and turned the feisty, sharp Maura into a dark and damaged shadow.

Exhaling, I pick up my phone and scroll through my contacts, my thumb hovering over her name. I haven't seen her since Adrian's funeral in May. Throughout the overbearing summer days working as a ranch hand on my uncle's farm, I thought of her often, even texting her a handful of times.

She never responded.

Maybe she knows?

No, no one knows the truth.

Although Maura and I spent a lot of time together, our friendship only existed through Adrian. In ways, losing him also meant losing her. She was a constant fixture in our dorm room and at this house last year. She rowed at the same regattas as us and always cheered for our boat.

We've crossed paths at the same parties, been to a few group dinners together, and I've slept at her family home more times than I can count, bumping into her on my way to the coffee pot in the morning.

Seeing her face in this photo, the angry slash of her eyebrows and twist of her mouth claws at something in my chest and eats at my stomach like acid.

I wish I could reach out and wrap her in my arms, squeeze her until all the desperation and sadness and anger leak out.

She'd probably swing at me for showing her concern. For even caring.

Chuckling, I close my laptop. Maura is a lot like her brother, tough and scrappy.

Massaging the space between my eyebrows, I look around my room.

The silence expands. Too many thoughts I don't want to consider sift through my mind.

Adrian. Adrian. Adrian.

Screw this.

Jumping up, I tug on some running shorts, grab my head-phones and SUV keys, and flee the space that once felt like home.

3

MAURA

S weat drips down the center of my back, causing my tank top to stick to my skin. Black curls escape Adrian's old baseball cap, blowing behind me as I pick up my pace.

Three miles into my run, my legs ache, my lower back throbs, and my lungs scream for relief. As much as my body cries for me to stop, I ignore it's warning signs and push on.

In a totally masochistic way, I remind myself that the ache is good. It's a reminder that I'm in training, working toward something, still alive. To distract myself, I take in the familiar sights along Boathouse Row.

I've spent countless hours here over the past three years. The trees are a summery green, the river full of shells and sculls. Runners, bikers, and in-line skaters pass by in shocks of energy, their workout gear colorful and bright.

At the four-and-a-half-mile marker, my shoelace unties, a hot pink lace flopping back and forth over my shoe with each step. Rolling my eyes at myself for not double-knotting my laces, I veer off the trail so I can stop to retie my shoe. As I slow to a jog, I step on the shoe lace and lunge forward, throwing my arms up to break my fall. Mere inches from hitting the ground, an arm shoots out and wraps around my waist, halting my faceplant.

"Oof." I slam into a wall of muscle. Breathing heavily, I lean forward, bracing my hands on my knees as the adrenaline of my near fall subsides. The strong arm lets go and I immediately miss it's hold, the twist of fingers in my tank top, the graze of a large palm along my hip. A shock of awareness shot through my body at his touch and even though I don't know him, my body craves the connection. Glancing up through a sweaty mass of curls, I croak, "Thanks for the save."

His back is to me as he walks a few steps ahead, his hands on his hips as he catches his breath. *Maybe he was doing sprints?* He's tall and lean with dirty blond, tousled hair. A pool of sweat darkens the red of his T-shirt, spreading out across broad shoulders and tapering along his waist. He nods at my "thanks" and turns around.

And my heart jumps into my throat.

"Zack?" My tone is more accusatory than grateful, and I wince as shock blooms in his expression.

"Maura? What are you doing here?"

I gesture toward my workout clothes.

Drinking in his tanned skin, full lips, and cerulean eyes, a spike of awareness travels through my veins, warming my blood. His jawline is carved from stone, his shoulders pulling the material of his T-shirt across his chest.

When the hell did Huntington become...hot?

"How are you doing, Maura?"

My heart gallops in my chest again and I work a swallow, certain the buzz thrumming in my veins is from his proximity and not my almost fall. And it pisses me off. Because it's just Zack. "Fine. Training starts tomorrow."

"Same. I just got back today." He bends to retrieve the

Toronto Blue Jays hat from the ground, a stricken look crossing his face as he turns the hat over in his hands, his thumb swiping across the worn stitching. "Here you go."

"Thanks." Our fingers brush and a surge of warmth, a moment of comfort, passes between us before I break the connection. Placing the cap between my knees, I retie my ponytail and try to act unaffected by the sight of him.

It's just Zack.

Adrian's best friend.

Hell, he was Adrian's shadow for his entire college career.

And yet, here he stands, full of life, while my brother is gone.

"How was your summer?" I bite out.

"Long. I worked as a ranch hand at my uncle's farm."

"Nebraska?"

He nods.

"Tough life, then? All work and no play?" My tone is condescending. My words harsh and unfair, but I don't care. Because Adrian is dead, and Zack is... here. He's acting normal, like we're old friends having a chat, when the truth is, we barely spoke outside of my brother's presence.

His gaze hardens, his Adam's apple bobbing in his throat. "My summer fucking sucked. You?"

I wince at his tone, shuffling back a step. Sometimes, I really am a bitch. But hey, at least I own it, right?

"Same." I pull the cap back on, tugging the brim lower so I can study Zack underneath its protection. He looks bigger, older, more mature than I remember. But then again, I never bothered to pay much attention to him. He was always Adrian's best friend, the brother he never had. But now, the way his shoulders stretch the material of his sweaty T-shirt, his biceps bunching as he clenches his fists, his blue eyes narrowed in on me, I realize that Zack Huntington is really fucking hot. Sure, I've always known he was a good-looking guy, but the Zack standing before me now, all grown-up and watching me, suddenly feels overwhelming, like he's stripping me bare. And more than just my clothes.

"I messaged you."

"I know." I force myself to meet his gaze. "I was busy."

"I just wanted to, you know, see how you're doing." His voice softens, a tenderness I don't want to accept wrapping around his words, flickering in his eyes.

"I'm fine."

"Maura."

"I'm fine, Zack. I don't need another brother looking out for me. Already had one of those and it didn't pan out that great."

Zack jerks back before hardening his gaze, an arctic blast blazing from his eyes. Instead of retreating, he steps closer.

Panic floods my chest as I read the genuine concern mixed with curiosity in his eyes, an understanding I don't like in the softness of his lips. *What the hell?* "Yeah. Listen, I gotta finish this run. Take care, Zack." I raise my hand in an awkward half-wave before turning on my heel and jogging down the trail.

"Maura, wait!"

Ignoring him, I run faster.

It takes me a quarter of a mile to realize I never tied my shoe.

4

ZACK

Maura's back recedes as she runs down the trail, her tiny blue shorts fluttering in the breeze. Adrian's lucky baseball hat on her head, a pink shoelace trailing her steps, everything about her is a contradiction.

One that pisses me off and draws me closer at the same damn time.

She's different than I remember, older somehow with Adrian's loss hanging around her like a shroud. Her gestures are quick, her lips twisted in sarcasm, her dark eyes bleeding pain. And running into her so unexpectedly after seeing her Facebook photo shocks my system. I did this to her; I turned a beautiful, smiling, sweet girl into the dark, edgy, damaged Maura who took off running the instant she realized I cared.

Calling it a day, I jog back in the direction of the boathouse.

It takes me longer to reach my car than it should. I'm lagging, but I couldn't care less. The sadness in Maura's eyes winded me more than sprints ever could.

Reaching my Land Rover, I unlock the door and slide into the driver's seat, picking up a warm bottle of water from the center console and drinking it anyway. Placing the key in the ignition, I'm about to start the engine when a flash of blue running shorts stops me.

She's three parking spots down, leaning against a white Range Rover, her back pressed against the door, one sneaker propped on the running board behind her. The Blue Jays hat is gone. Her hair is down now, a sheet of wild black curls. Her body is tight; long, lean legs, a slender waist, hips I'd like to sink my fingertips into and grip. Maura's always had wicked curves but now, she's got an attitude to match. Her skin glistens in the sunlight, her eyes too dark and too far away for me to read. Nonetheless, an edge wraps around her like an aura, drawing attention like a warning sign. *Proceed with caution.*

A guy steps to her, tall, beefy, and loud. The left side of his neck is inked, tattoos disappearing underneath his white wife-beater. Stepping closer, he squeezes her hips, sliding his palms up to her tiny waist. A growl rips from my chest as anger boils my blood.

Who the hell is this guy?

Maura laughs loudly, too loudly. Even through my windshield, I notice her discomfort. Her body is wound too tight, her neck stiff, her shoulders bunched. The guy turns, two teardrop tattoos under his left eye jumping out from his skin.

What the fuck, Maura?

Even I, Zackary Huntington from Nowhere, Nebraska, know that teardrop tattoos represent a murder committed, time in prison, or the loss of a loved one. And judging by this guy's build, stature, and tough-guy attitude, I'm ruling out option three.

Jerking the handle of my SUV, I step onto the asphalt. Maura notices me immediately, her eyes widening as panic crosses her face.

What the hell has she gotten herself into?

Why is she even talking to this clown?

Come on, Rodriguez, Adrian would want so much more for you.

The guy notices her reaction because he begins to turn toward me when Maura reaches out, running her hands up his arms and locking her fingers behind his meaty neck. She pouts adorably, and I clench my hand into a fist as desire floods through me.

When the hell did she become so sexy?

Why am I even noticing?

And when did she start hanging out with hardened guys from the neighborhood she grew up in?

He steps to her, and she glares at me over his shoulder. Her message is clear: *get out of here.* I shake my head, glaring back.

The corner of her mouth twitches as she palms his cheek, guiding his face down to hers. She kisses him slowly, her lips parting, her tongue dancing against his. It's sensual and sexual and intense.

It's heady and potent and so fucking wrong.

Anger burns in the pit of my stomach, surging through my veins like lava.

Maura's eye glitter with mockery; she stares at me the entire time.

"YO, HUNTINGTON, YOU HUNGRY?" Damien D'Arco calls out as I walk into the house.

"Yeah, man. What're you thinking?" I stand near the stairs leading to mine and Hunt's bedrooms, my arm dangling off the top of the banister.

"Burgers and beers? Might as well enjoy a few brews before Coach forces us to go dry."

"Yeah, sounds good. Give me ten; I need to shower."

"Sweet." Damien stretches his legs out in front of him on the floor, his back resting against the couch. He picks up an Xbox controller and resumes whatever game he's playing.

Hopping into the shower, I rinse off quickly, the hot water loosening the stiffness in my legs and back. After toweling off, I pull on a pair of ripped jeans and a black Henley. Combing my fingers through my wet hair, I pull it up into a manbun.

"D'Arco! Let's roll," I call out to Damien as I slip into a pair of flip flops I forgot just inside the front door.

"Coming, bro." He walks out of the kitchen, grabbing a set of car keys from the top of the microwave. Hunt and Bilson follow, and the four of us make our way outside, piling into Damien's Hummer, which we've all pointed out— several times—is the stupidest SUV to drive in the cramped streets and severely limited parking options of Philadelphia. Damien disagrees, convinced that his monstrosity gets him girls.

It doesn't.

Damien navigates through the city traffic to Billows, a pub we frequent when we're not dry or trying to cut weight. After parking the Hummer several streets away, we make it inside, and Hunt's eyes cut straight to the bar to check out the talent.

"Candace is here."

Bilson groans. "Not this again. Dude, let it go. She turned you down nicely."

"That was last semester." Hunt points out. "She broke up with that douchebag she was seeing over the summer."

D'Arco chuckles at Hunt's reasoning, lifting an eyebrow. "I don't know, man; I think she could do better than you."

"Is that a bet?"

"Is what a bet?" Bilson's eyebrows knit together. "I told you to let it go."

"It sounded like a bet." Hunt flips his chin to D'Arco.

"Yeah, man. If you can pick her up tonight, I'll cover your burger and all the beers you can drink," D'Arco tells him.

Hunt ponders the offer, his face serious before his smile cuts through. "You're on."

"Get a table." Bilson pushes Hunt forward, away from the bar.

The rest of us trail behind, sliding into a corner booth. We order a round of beers and some wings to start. While we wait for our apps, Hunt's eyes stray back to the bar, back to Candace. "Hey," he says suddenly, his eyes flashing to mine. "Lauren's here."

Bilson groans out loud. "Does every outing with you have to be about scoring with some random girl?"

"Hell yeah. And Candace isn't random." He turns toward me. "Come up to the bar with me, Huntington. Just keep Lauren entertained for like ten minutes, give me some time to chat up Candace."

Lauren Layton.

My ex-girlfriend.

We dated my entire sophomore and half of my junior year. And yeah, for a stretch of time, I thought she was the one. Long brown hair that falls down her back in waves, deep blue eyes I could get lost in, a slamming body. She's always been beautiful. Sweet too. But even though we had insane chemistry in between the sheets, we lacked a deeper connection outside of the bedroom. You know that borderline obsession of not being able to breathe without the other person?

Yeah, that was never there for us.

After Adrian passed, Lauren reached out. Several times. I just wasn't feeling it, not feeling her. How could I drag someone so sweet into the mess I've made of my life?

But right now, after being rattled by my encounter with Maura Rodriguez, the old familiarity and comfort of the past is inviting.

Lauren Layton.

I'd be all for tangling up with her again. For a little while anyway. Like tonight.

Unbidden, Maura's blue running shorts, her dark and dangerous eyes, the angry slant of her mouth flashes through my mind and my throat dries.

What the hell is wrong with me?

I can't think of Maura like that. She's Adrian's sister. That's a violation of bro code, even if Adrian isn't here to kick my ass.

My eyes cut back to Lauren. Her skinny jeans hug her hips perfectly, a white sleeveless shirt shows off her tanned shoulders, and her familiar laugh reaches my ears as she lifts a hand to cover her nose. A sweet gesture, one I've seen her do a thousand times.

Nostalgia sticks to the edges of a hundred old memories from sophomore year. *Adrian encouraging me to ask Lauren out. The three of us drinking beers in Love Park. Adrian busting my balls about writing Lauren a poem for our anniversary.* It all comes flooding back. In hindsight, it all seems so innocent, sweet.

"Sure, man." I nod at Hunt. "I'll wingman you."

"Careful, Huntington." D'Arco warns. "You dodged a bullet when you ended things with Lauren."

"What are you talking about?"

"Just saying, she was desperate to get back together with you. Probably still is."

"It's just one night." Hunt frowns at D'Arco, pulling me from the booth.

Bilson swears.

5

MAURA

Hector's stubble scratches the inside of my thighs as his head dips lows. The ceiling in his bedroom has a long crack bisecting one corner with little lines shooting off in haphazard directions. He should really get that fixed. His walls are bare: no pictures, posters, or flags pinned anywhere. Nothing to show that he lives here; maybe no one does.

"You like that, baby?" he rasps, his lips murmuring against my hip as he works his way up my body.

I moan appropriately.

He runs his fingers up my ribcage, over my chest, circling his palm at the base of my throat. "Maura," he says, his dark eyes intent on mine. "You sure about this?"

Oh fuck!

What, he's going to be thoughtful and considerate now?

One of the reasons I like hooking up with Hector is because he doesn't give a shit about anyone except himself. Things with him are easy, uncomplicated, straightforward. We hookup and then we go our separate ways until one of us needs a warm and willing body to get lost in again. Now, after weeks of random late nights and drunken, hazy hookups, he asks me if I want it?

I blink, noting the water spot on the wall over his right shoulder. I doubt he lives here.

Am I at a room where he and his buddies take girls to bang?

That thought almost depresses me before I remember the purpose of my visit.

"Yeah." My eyelids fall closed as Hector pushes into me.

Turn off the feelings, turn off the thoughts.

Block out everything except this moment.

Except my phone chirps with a new message and my curiosity piques.

Is Mia texting her favorite gelato flavors? Did Lila already hook up with a surfer? Is Emma sending articles about female empowerment through sports?

Or is it Mom? Maybe one of my aunts?

"God, Maura, you feel so fucking good."

Gripping Hector's shoulders, scoring his back with my fingernails, I block out my wayward thoughts. When Hector's spent, he rolls off of me and triumph fills my chest.

See, I can forget for a while. All I need is a good distraction.

Except when I check my phone, my feel-good buzz withers and dies like a plucked dandelion.

Zack: Good seeing you, Rodriguez. If you need anything, I'm here. Always.

IT'S LATE when I enter my dorm room.

Or early, depending on how you perceive time. For me, 2:00 AM is crazy late since I need to be at the boathouse at

5:00 AM. Hungover, sore, and exhausted are definitely not how I wanted to begin my last season at McShain. Crawling into bed, I pull the duvet over my shoulders, close my eyes, and will sleep to come quickly.

Briiiing.

The shrill sound of my alarm cuts through the air seconds later and I groan, scrubbing a palm over my face.

Should I just ditch practice?

Would it even matter?

An image of Adrian pops into my head, his crooked smile and mischievous eyes. He loved the beginning of the season, the first day back on the water, the first moment when the boat seems to fly, everyone in unison after months apart.

Checking my phone, I scan the messages.

Mia: Good luck today, Maura!

Lila: Any hot new recruits on the men's team? Keep an eye out!

Emma: Bitches best watch out because you're back on the water today!

Zack: Good luck today.

Cursing, I roll out of bed and pull on a pair of shorts and a tank top. Tucking my hair under one of Adrian's baseball caps, I hide the heavy bags under my eyes behind sunglasses and head to the boathouse.

What the hell is Zack doing texting me?

Acting like we're best friends and he somehow understands?

The cool air feels good as I walk the city streets, soothing my temper and calming my nerves. Walking to the boathouse before sunrise has always been my favorite moment of the day: breezes tickling my shoulders and calves, shadows hiding my footsteps, my breath the only sound in the quiet. It's like the state between waking and dreaming, a moment of solitude before daybreak, peace before chaos. When I leave the boathouse later this morning, the sun will be blazing, people filling the streets, and the quiet will cease to exist. But in this moment, it's like the city belongs to me.

Jogging the last few steps to the boathouse door, I note that the team bus has already arrived.

"Hey, Rodriguez."

"Maura, good to see you!"

"Hey, how was your summer?"

My teammates, the girls I've spent the last three years learning from, improving with, confiding in, envelop me in hugs and high fives. I grin when I'm supposed to, ask the right questions, crack jokes like usual, but it's forced. Nothing is easy or smooth or natural. These days, nothing feels normal.

"You good, girl?" Valerie, our stroke seat, asks gently.

"Yeah, ready to get the season started!" I throw an arm around her neck. "But I totally dropped the ball on conditioning."

"Me too. These next few weeks are gonna be brutal."

"Same."

"At least we're in it together."

"Exactly."

In the past, it was true. These girls and I, we were always in it together. Whatever "it" was. I could count on them and they could lean on me and we would sort it out. But now they could never understand; we're not in "it" together. I'm all alone, floating out in the choppy, destructive, dangerous waters of the open sea, half-hoping I don't drown, half-praying I do.

Fifteen minutes later our boat is rigged, and we're back on the water, our oars slicing through the river, our bodies bending in sync. As if we never left. As if nothing has changed. As if the finale of last season, Adrian's death, never occurred.

My final season has started.

And my heart's too damaged to care.

THE FIRST WEEK of training shreds my palms, causes my back muscles to spasm, makes my legs burn. I'm so sore I can hardly move, collapsing into bed each night, too exhausted to think, too beat to dream.

And for that I'm grateful, because the only thing worse than dreaming about Adrian's death, waking with my heart in my throat and tear stains on my pillowcase, is dreaming about Adrian's life, waking up happy only to remember.

And then I have to search out the clammy claws of numbness all over again. These days, I only find it at the bottom of a bottle or underneath Hector's sweaty frame.

For the first time in a long time, rowing seems like a gift again and not a prison, shackling me to memories of my twin.

SEPTEMBER

6

ZACK

The start of the season is always tough.

Physically, it's debilitating. Mentally, it's exhausting. Emotionally, well, you have to dig deep. Still, after each practice, each session in the gym, even each study hall, there's a sense of satisfaction. A feeling of contentment.

But this year, all of it is just painful.

Leaving the library on Monday afternoon, I pull out my phone and debate sending Maura another text. She's hardcore blowing me off which has me more concerned than I care to admit.

Is she okay?

Who was the guy from the parking lot?

Is she in trouble?

Stop thinking about Maura.

Adrian would want you to look out for his sister.

"Zack!" My name cuts through the air, and I stop to wait for whoever is trailing me across the quad.

Turning, I grin when I see Lauren.

She looks beautiful, her long hair pulled back from her face, a sundress skimming her toned thighs, and pink toenails winking with each step. Just two weeks ago, those toned thighs wrapped around my waist, her hair splayed out across my pillow, as her toenails curled into my back.

"Hey, babe." The endearment falls from my lips as naturally as the sun rising.

"Hi. Where're you heading?" She falls in step beside me.

I slip my arm around her waist, my fingertips stroking her flat stomach. "Urban Housing with Kowalski. You?"

"Organic Chemistry." Her mouth twists. "I'm going to fail."

I chuckle, pulling her closer into my side. She still fits perfectly. "You're not going to fail. It's September. You've got plenty of time to make up for the B you probably got on the one and only quiz you've taken so far."

"How'd you know?"

"'Cause I know you."

She grins, her hand catching the back of my shirt, her fingers twisting the material. "True."

I pat her hip reassuringly as we reach the Architecture building. "This is me."

"Zack, I ..." She fiddles with the pendant on her necklace: two interlinking hearts I gave her at the end of sophomore year.

"What is it?"

"I miss you." She glances up, a flicker of insecurity in her blue eyes. "I miss us."

My fingers catch the ends of her hair, the scent of cinnamon enveloping me. Nodding, I stall, unsure of what to say. Sure, I miss her sometimes. She's the sweetest, most genuine person I know. And when she reached out in the wake of Adrian's passing, I shut her down. Hard.

But now, with her standing before me, vulnerability and

trust in her gaze, I want to go back to sophomore year when everything was easy. Simple.

I want to go back to before.

"Me too," I tell her, and I mean it. "How about we go for dinner tomorrow night? You still obsessed with sushi?"

She lets out a small breath, her relief evident as a smile spreads across her mouth. "I'd love to," she pops onto her toes and kisses my cheek. "Sushi sounds perfect."

"I'll pick you up at 7:00 PM."

"I'll be ready."

"Later, babe."

Turning into the Architecture building, I locate my classroom and slide behind a desk thirty seconds before Kowalski introduces himself. The whole lecture, my thoughts ping-pong between the cinnamon sweetness of Lauren and the sexy spice of Maura.

"NICE WORK TODAY." Phillips, our captain, tosses over his shoulder as we walk back into the boathouse.

"Thanks, man. You too." I stretch my arms overhead and try not to wince at the soreness rippling down my spine, cutting into my ribcage.

"I mean it; the boat felt lighter. Not like it was but we're getting there."

Not like it was.

Because Adrian is gone. And nothing is like it was.

"Yeah."

"Heard you're hanging with Lauren again."

"Who'd you hear that from?"

Phillips shrugs. "Marissa and I are having a party on Friday. Nothing crazy. Just wine and cheese or whatever." He smiles sheepishly. The guy is practically engaged. "You guys should come."

"Cool, man. We'll see."

"Catch you later, then."

"'Bye." I shoulder my duffel bag and walk back to my SUV.

Flipping the ignition, I shoot off a quick text.

Me: Maura, just let me know you're okay? How's practice going?

The line of my unanswered messages mocks me, but I don't care. I already carry around enough guilt for a Rodriguez sibling; I'm not going to add another.

7

MAURA

The scotch is strong and smooth as it coats my throat.

Holding the glass casually, I watch the single ice cube melt. Until last month, I'd never had scotch before; now it's a weekly vice. At least, this week.

"It's from Scotland," the man sitting across from me explains. His hair is dark. He leaves it long. It's the type of hair a girl can run her fingers through, hold on to. Kind of like Zack's.

Where the hell did that thought pop up from?

Dismissing it, I run my eyes over the man. Even though he dresses young and casual in dark-washed jeans and a black button-down, I know he's pushing forty. He blinks steadily behind thick-framed glasses.

Does he wear them because he needs them or ironically, cashing in on a passing fad?

He watches me closely, drinking in every detail.

I nod, as if his words mean something.

They don't.

"It's smooth," I say.

A ghost of a smile shadows his lips as he continues to

watch me, his gaze perusing my body, pausing at my chest. I fight the urge to roll my eyes. So typical. Instead, I arch my back, pushing my chest out so he can appreciate my boobs in all their glory. The desire that heats his gaze doesn't disappoint and encourages me to move this exchange along.

"Are you in Philly for business or pleasure?" It comes out like a purr. I nearly roll my eyes at myself, my mind wandering back to just one year ago when Emma and Lila had to push me to approach a guy at the bar, had to coach me on what to say, how to act. Sometimes it surprises me that I've perfected this persona in such a short amount of time. If I wasn't so desperate to feel nothing, I might feel proud.

"Business." He arches an eyebrow. "But I'm not above mixing the two."

"Good."

"I'm at the Rittenhouse. Room 112." He slides a key card across the bar.

What type of business does a guy like him have in Philadelphia that has him staying at the Rittenhouse?

Ah, who cares?

Tapping the card twice, his fingers stray from the bar to caress the inside of my wrist. "Join me." It's not a question, it's a command.

An unexpected spark of excitement runs through me. A thrill. Finally, a feeling I can tolerate; it usually precedes the emptiness I crave.

"I'd love to." I palm the card, slipping it into my clutch.

"Good." He leans back on his barstool and picks up his scotch. A thick wedding band winks from his left finger.

I pretend not to see it.

And I know he will remove it before we make it to his hotel room. In the short amount of time I've been picking up complete strangers for the night, usually preferring the ease of Hector, I've learned that the married men always remove their wedding rings.

Sometimes denial is its own brand of pleasure.

"RODRIGUEZ! ARE YOU OKAY?" Kay Hillard, our team captain, asks as she peers over the tops of her sunglasses. Her eyes narrow, a mixture of concern and frustration swimming in their hazel depths.

"Fine." Clearing my throat, I grin. My head throbs, my heartbeat pounds in my temples. Freaking scotch. "I'm fine." My go-to words these days: I'm fine, everything's fine, it's fine.

"You don't look fine." Amber Mason throws in as she braids her hair, fastening the end with a silver hair tie.

I cut her a look but quickly rearrange my features; it's best not to show a reaction. Any reaction. I wave my hand. "Just getting over a cold. Really, I'm fine."

Kay nods her head curtly, but she doesn't look convinced. Clapping her hands twice, she secures the attention of the other girls in the Varsity Eight, as we form a half moon around her. "How did today feel?"

Valerie shakes her head. "Something's off with the start. We're too slow."

Our coxswain, Amanda Stevens, nods in agreement. The rest of the girls chime in with their thoughts, their opinions. Everyone but me.

I'm too busy thinking about last night, too distracted remembering the way his hands felt on my skin. The way he trailed his fingertips up my ribcage with purpose, intent, peeling my shirt off in the process. The way he kissed my neck, his lips pressed against my clavicle, his breath tickling my cheek. How he sounded panting in my ear, begging me for more, begging me. He had a fallen angel tattoo on his left shoulder blade, and he smelled like soap and scotch. Like a man. Like all the men.

"Rodriguez." Kay's voice snaps me back to the present.

"Yeah?"

"Do you have anything to add?"

"Nope."

She sighs and I hear all the words she's not saying: *What the hell is wrong with you?* But after a hard look, Kay turns to listen to Valerie's additional suggestions about our start.

Our Varsity Eight is currently ranked number two in the US. For most of us, it's our last season to row, to compete, to be number one. And everyone, especially Kay Hillard, is one thousand percent committed to making this season—our final season—our best yet.

I wish I cared. I used to care. I used to care more than anyone, including Kay. Turning my heavy sigh into a cough, I recall the way his fingers felt digging into my scalp, tugging hard at my hair.

I peek at my Fitbit to check the time. 7:38 AM. Practice should wrap up any minute. I have an 8:00 AM class. Photography. Craning my neck to the right, I feel a delicious tingle that travels down my shoulder and arm. I'm sore from last night and it feels good, fulfilling. He was fulfilling.

Kay claps her hands again, signaling the end of practice. Tossing my practice duffle over my shoulder, my back aches, reminding me of his bruising touch, his unbridled passion.

Too tired to walk home today, I climb the steps onto the team bus and scan the rows before taking an empty seat on the left. Turning toward the window, I pop in my earbuds and choose a random playlist from Spotify.

He had large, rough, calloused hands that sent chills up

my spine and unleashed butterflies in the pit of my stomach when he touched me. Pulling my hair out of its ponytail and combing my fingers through my tangled mass of curls, his scent engulfs me once more. It's heady and wild and complicated.

I wish I remembered his name.

8

ZACK

My hand rests in the dip above Lauren's ass, my fingers itching to slide south as I guide her into Phillips' and Marissa's townhouse. They own a brownstone a few blocks from campus in the ritzy area of Rittenhouse Square, compliments of Phillips' grandmother. As nice as it is to see my friend in a relationship with a great girl, I can't help but wonder if he would be so "in love" with Marissa if his whole family wasn't pushing for an engagement. It's a lot of pressure for a twenty-two-year-old to wrap his head around. I mean, who the hell hosts a wine and cheese night in college anyway?

I guess that's the way of things when your father owns a tech company and her father is a senator. Politics suck.

"We're here," Lauren calls out as she pushes into their townhouse.

I let my fingers slide down her ass as she steps forward. After our dinner date on Tuesday ended with breakfast in bed Wednesday morning, I'm relieved, maybe even happy, that she's back in my life.

"Yay!" Marissa squeals, enveloping Lauren in a warm

hug. She's wearing a brightly colored paisley-printed dress. Like the Lily Pulitzer shit Nicole always scoffs at. Phillips better go into politics because Marissa would make the perfect congressman's wife.

I cough through my laughter. I really need to call my sister.

"Zackary, you're looking well." Marissa kisses my cheek, patting my shoulder with her palm.

I will not roll my eyes. "You too, Maris." Her nose wrinkles at the nickname.

Is it messed up that I take pleasure in her discomfort? Probably.

"Hey, man," Phillips calls from the kitchen as we make our way into the living room. The brownstone really is beautiful with an open-concept floorplan, huge windows, and high ceilings. It's what most couples would aspire to buy in their thirties. Phillips just beat them to it. "Want a beer?" He comes around the corner and holds out a Stella.

"Marcus!" Marissa scolds. "We're doing wine and cheese."

Phillips shrugs, his arm shrinking back. Before it can retract completely, and take the beer with it, I swipe the bottle from his hand. "A beer would be great. Thanks."

Marissa turns away, tugging Lauren's hand. "Come on, I'll pour us some wine. Everyone should arrive in the next half hour, so it gives us a chance to catch up."

"How's it going?" I ask Phillips.

"All good." He rubs the back of his neck. "Hey, you mind taking a walk around the corner with me? I forgot to pick up ice. And as much as Marissa wants this to be all about wine and cheese, I'm sure the guys will want real drinks."

Of course the guys will want real drinks. We officially go dry in the spring semester, so the fall is our only chance to enjoy college. "Let's go." I place the beer bottle down on an end table and try not to wince as Phillips slips a coaster beneath it. Seriously?

"Marissa, we're going to grab ice," he calls out.

"Okay." Her voice is shrill.

Phillips' shoulders tighten imperceptibly as I follow him out of the brownstone and down the stairs leading to the street.

"How're things with Lauren going?" he asks as we hit the pavement.

"Good. I mean, she's a great girl. Things between us, they're never complicated, you know?"

"There's a lot of history there."

"Exactly."

We cross the street, passing by the Rittenhouse Hotel. A girl turns in front of the entrance, her dark curls fluttering in the wind before settling around her shoulders. She smiles, her palms sliding up her boyfriend's arms, her fingers locking behind his neck. And the gesture is shockingly familiar. As is the girl.

"Is that Maura Rodriguez?"

Damn it, Maura. What are you doing?

"Uh, I don't know. Doesn't really look like her."

"Yeah, man. That's totally her. Who is she with?" Phillips veers off the sidewalk, closer to the hotel. "Shit, that guy's old."

Fuck!

"Maura!" he calls out.

She jumps back from the man as if she's been electro-cuted. Noticing Phillips, her arms drop to her sides. "Hi, Marcus."

"What are you doing here?" Phillips keeps at it, walking up to the hotel entrance.

"Just catching up with a friend." She gestures toward the man standing next to her. The man old enough to be her father.

Anger blazes in my veins, a protectiveness surging in my blood. *Is he taking advantage of her? Is he propositioning her? Or is she actually into him?*

"Your wife must be pretty awesome, letting you have twenty-one-year-old friends." I seethe, my eyes boring holes into the old dude's skull.

Maura gasps beside me but I ignore her.

A wave of uncertainty washes over the man's features as he steps back, his eyes cutting to his watch. "Sorry, Maura. I have to go. Good, uh, you know, good seeing you." He turns around quickly, slipping his left hand into his pocket.

I turn toward Maura but she regards me coolly. Her stance is defiant, her arms crossed in front of her chest. "Really?" she quirks an eyebrow.

"Who is he?"

"A friend."

"How'd you meet him?"

"Zack, stop. You're overreacting. I've gotta head back to campus anyway. Good seeing you guys." She dismisses me, turning away. Her black skirt inches up her thighs with each step she takes.

"Maura, wait," Phillips calls out, cutting me a look.

She pauses, as if considering if she should turn around or not. Eventually, she turns, staring at Phillips expectantly.

"Marissa and I are having some friends over. Wine and cheese. Come with us." He walks toward Maura and rests his arm around her shoulders. "We miss seeing you."

Discomfort rolls off Maura and radiates from her pores.

"If you have other plans, I'll walk you home." I offer, giving her an out. Besides, I'd love to have some alone time with Maura to ask her what the hell she's doing with her life and why she's ignoring all of my messages.

"Nah, man. Maura's coming with us." Phillips decides, dragging Maura along.

She ignores me completely.

9

MAURA

Zack's eyes burn the space between my shoulder blades as I shuffle next to Marcus.

After hooking up with the DILF from the Rittenhouse Hotel, I replaced Hector with him every night this week. Scotch and sex never tasted so good.

Except now, Zack knows.

Zack, who keeps sending me thoughtful messages.

Zack, who looks at me like he knows I'm falling apart inside.

And, even worse, like he cares.

Stepping into Marcus's brownstone, my eyebrows shoot up when I see Lauren.

I snicker and Zack stiffens beside me.

Is she the type of woman Zack likes?

Sweet and compliant?

"Maura, I'm so sorry for your loss. How are you holding up?" Lauren pulls me into a hug, her voice dripping with sympathy.

And I want to punch her.

Right in her beautiful face.

"I'm fine. You?" I muffle into her thick mane of hair.

"Good, thanks. It's so good to see you." She leans back, peering into my face, one hand still clasping my shoulder. "I didn't even know you were coming tonight! Zack, you should have told me." She turns toward Zack, slipping her other arm around his waist and pulling him into our little circle.

Zack flashes me a look I can't read before opening his mouth.

"It was a last-minute thing," I cut in smoothly. "I'm going to grab a drink. Can I bring you anything?" I look from Lauren to Zack, desperate to make my getaway.

"I'm good." Lauren lifts her wine glass from the end table.

"Me too." Zack bites out, his tone frosty.

I escape to the kitchen just as the front door swings open and more members from the LaFarge crew team and their plus ones enter the brownstone. Swiping a beer, I search for a place to hide.

Not much time passes before Zack finds me, sitting on top of Marcus's dryer in the laundry room. Swinging my legs in time with the music, I sip my beer and peel the label on the carton of Tide beside me.

"Avoiding me?" His deep voice startles me.

"You know, not everything is about you, Huntington."

"Then why the animosity?" He enters the room and partially closes the door, leaving it cracked for more light and sound to enter.

"Why the messages?"

He chuckles. "That's what this is about? You're pissed at me for caring about you?"

"You never cared before." I challenge, biting the inside of my cheek because —

"That's bullshit. I've always cared about you. You're Adrian's sister, I've always looked out —"

"For my best interests?" I raise an eyebrow, taking a gulp of beer.

"What are you doing with the men?" He slides next to me on the dryer, shifting me over until I'm half on the washing machine.

"The men?"

"Yeah. You know, the thug and the married man?"

"Judgmental much?"

"Answer the goddamn question."

"I'm having fun, Zack. Jesus, my twin died. I'm blowing off steam, trying to enjoy my life. Is that okay with you?"

"No, Maura, it's not." Zack's voice hardens, an arctic blast swirling in his eyes. "Because you're not blowing off steam. This isn't fucking spring break; this is your life."

"Oh, and now you're going to tell me how to live it?" I slip off the washing machine/dryer. "I'm not interested in the unsolicited advice."

"I care about you." His voice is quiet, a hint of desperation wrapping around his words.

Keeping my back to him, I stare into the light of the party. "Why?"

"Because I miss you, Maura."

Snorting, I shake my head. "Zack, we've never really been —"

"Don't say we've never been friends. We've always been something more than this."

Spinning around, I shake my head at him. "Zack —"

"I miss him, Maura. Every goddamn day, I miss him. And you may be the only person in the world who can come close to understanding how I feel. And vice versa. Stop shutting me out. Stop ignoring my messages. Stop blowing me off and be my fucking friend."

Zack tugs at the back of his neck in frustration. Sliding off the dryer, he stands in front of me, solid and reliable and…here. His hand cups my shoulder and gives it a shake. "What the hell is going on with you?"

Sarcasm burns the tip of my tongue, angry quips run through my mind but when I open my mouth, the most unexpected thing pops out. "Did Adrian ever tell you about our family trips to the beach in Wildwood, New Jersey?"

"Yeah." His brow furrows in confusion.

"We would spend all day in and out of the ocean, boogie-boarding, making sand castles, collecting sea shells. At night we would go on all the rides at the boardwalk. I loved the spinning tea cups best. You know what his favorite ride was? The Ferris Wheel." I chuckle and the sincerity behind it surprises me.

"The Ferris Wheel? That's not even a ride."

"It was to him. He said it was like being on top of the world and pausing time. You know, when you get stuck on top? It's like you're the only person who can see everything happening for those few moments until the ride starts again. It's just you and the air and the sky and everything that's happening below you isn't real. There's a disconnect."

"I guess."

"I'm stuck, Zack. It's been for longer than a few moments and I don't think the ride is ever going to start again."

Zack shuffles forward, crowding me. If I reach up, my palms will graze his abdomen, trail up his chest. "You have to try, Maura."

"What if I don't want to?" I glance up, noting the concern and compassion in his gaze, the tightness of his jaw, the severity of his expression.

"Then, I'll make you."

"Why?"

"Because I care about you. I always have."

10

ZACK

M aura Rodriguez breaks my heart.

Hearing her confession is like being punched underwater and knowing you can't inhale. Her words cause my throat to burn, my chest to constrict.

Being with her in the laundry room is like being wrapped up in a cocoon. Despite the party unfolding on the other side of the door, the only person I see in this moment is Maura.

And she's broken.

Tugging her against my chest, I wrap my arms around her. She gasps, her shoulders stiffening under my touch before she relaxes, melting into me.

"The ride is going to start again, Rodriguez. Maybe not this week or hell, even this year, but you're not going to be stuck forever. I promise."

"How do you know that?" she tips her face up, her eyes shining with a vulnerability she rarely shows.

"Because I won't let you stay stuck forever." I cup her cheek in my palm, swiping my thumb across her cheekbone.

Her skin heats under my touch and my eyes dip to her full

mouth, her soft lips. The space between us sizzles with an energy, a current, that was never there before.

"You know, for someone I've been ignoring, you're pretty confident about your place in my life."

Grinning, I drop my forehead to hers. "Maura, I was never going to give up on you. I just would have kept messaging."

"Stalker much?"

"Stop deflecting. Just, let me in. Let me be your friend. When you need to talk, call me. When you need to vent, confide in me. I'm right here, Maura, and I'm not going anywhere. So, use me."

I break eye contact, a blush creeping up my neck. If only he knew all the ways I want to use him. Get lost in him. "Won't that cause problems for you?"

"What?"

"With Lauren."

"Lauren and I aren't together. We're —"

"What are you doing in here?" The door swings open and Lauren enters. Her tone is accusatory, her eyes narrowed.

"Just shooting the shit," Maura says, stepping away from me. "Care to join?" She tilts her head toward the dryer.

"Um, no thanks. I was just looking for Zack." Lauren's gaze flips to me. "Marissa was just telling the funniest story about us sophomore year." She giggles and it's breathless. "Come on, you've got to hear it." She tugs my hand.

Glancing at Maura, all of the emotions that were swimming in her eyes moments ago disappeared. She grins but the softness is gone. Instead, the edge is back, erasing the traces of the old Maura. "I've got to get going. Nice seeing you, Lauren." Maura catches Lauren in a half-hug. "See you around, Zack," she calls to me over her shoulder.

By the time Lauren laces her fingers with mine and pulls me out of the laundry room, Maura is gone.

THAT NIGHT LAUREN'S hair spills over my pillow and her lips press kisses along my collarbone as I hover over her. She moans my name, digs her nails into my shoulders, presses her heels into my lower back. She arches into me, tells me how she wants it, and it is so good I can't see straight. But when the ecstasy subsides and I drift back to my pillow and blink, it's Maura's face and not hers.

I am completely fucked.

11

MAURA

ZACK: GO MINI-GOLFING WITH ME TODAY.

M*e: Why?*
Zack: Why not?

Zack: Aid and I used to go. Kinda in the mood for it and no one to go with. Take pity on me? (Crying face emoji)

I snort at the emoji.

Should I go?

I mean, it's Zack. Hot Zack with a killer body and piercing blue eyes, who keeps witnessing me shame it up with different men.

Friend Zack who is right; he probably does come the closest to understanding how I feel about Adrian's death.

Who even goes mini-golfing these days?

Me: Sure. 1:00 PM?

Zack: Pick you up then.

Even though I'm not one to try to impress a guy, I take extra time getting ready for my friend-date with Zack.

Lame, I know.

But still, I do it.

If Lila or Emma were here, the most perfect outfit would already be waiting on my bed. If Mia were here, she would offer encouraging words. My friends would support my foray back into the land of the living.

I could call them, but I don't want to. As if telling them will turn mini-golf with Zack into more than it is.

And it's nothing.

Still, I tame my long, wild curls into beach waves that hang to the small of my back. I add a second coat of mascara to my lashes and opt for lip gloss over Chapstick. Okay, so nothing major, but for me, this is as complicated as glamming gets.

After trying on and discarding most of my closet, I settle on a pair of well-worn ripped jeans that hug my ass spectacularly and a dangerously low V-neck black tissue tee. I tuck in the front of the shirt on the side so it hangs casually. Adding a pair of stud earrings and a long necklace I swiped from Lila, I slide into sandals and am ready to go.

Checking myself out in the floor-length mirror on the back of my door, I look good. I mean, I know that I'm physically in shape and have some decent facial attributes, but it's more than that. My cheeks are flushed, nearly glowing. My eyes are bigger, brighter than they have been in a long time. I almost look happy.

I scowl.

Zack: Here.

Taking a deep breath, I roll my eyes at my reflection and grab my purse from its permanent home on the floor.

Zack's gray Land Rover glints in the sunshine as I walk down the path leading from my dorm to the parking lot. The windows are open, his arm slung casually out the window, fingertips tapping a beat I can't discern against the door. He waves when he sees me, a slow smile spreading across his lips.

Damn. He's sexy.

I lift my fingers in a half-wave and try to lessen the sashay of my hips that beg for his attention, for him to notice me, to want me. Ugh. He's Adrian's best friend!

He reaches over the center console and opens the passenger door for me, and I nearly swoon. He passed The Door Test. Just like in *A Bronx Tale*. Mine and Adrian's favorite movie. If this was any other guy, you know, not Adrian's best friend—and if Adrian was still alive—we would discuss this gesture at length. And then watch the movie, eating a bag of mixed cheddar and caramel popcorn with Skittles thrown in like we used to.

Shaking the past from my mind, I climb into the SUV. "Hey." A suitable greeting for a non-date.

Zack smiles.

And my insides melt.

12

ZACK

The sight of Maura leaves me temporarily speechless as she walks over to my SUV from her dorm room. She looks good. Real good. Like I want to wake up next to her tomorrow and cook her breakfast in bed good.

Shit, I clench my fingers into a fist. This isn't supposed to happen. I can't like Maura, be into Maura of all girls. That's almost as bad as wanting Amelia, Adrian's ex-girlfriend from freshman year.

With each step Maura takes, a thin sliver of her black bra shows as the neckline of her T-shirt dips. Her jeans are skintight, painted onto her perfectly sculpted body. Her hair is long, the color of midnight, and I try real fucking hard not to imagine it wrapped around my forearm, fisted in my fingers.

To distract myself, I lean over to open the passenger door for her. And then she smiles at me and time literally stops. *Get it together, Zack. This is Maura. Adrian's little sister.*

"Hey," she mutters and it's clear that I have no effect on her, which helps snap me back to reality.

"How's it goin'?"

She shrugs, a flash of her black satin bra showing as she

clicks in her seatbelt. "You know, same old. You and Adrian, you used to do this a lot?" She gestures toward the dashboard, but I know what she's asking: *did you and my brother really go mini-golfing?*

"Yeah, we did." I put the car in reverse and back out of the spot, turning to exit the parking lot. "It started at the end of freshman year. We were so freaking bored during spring break. All of our friends were partying it up in Mexico or the DR, and here we were, two shmucks killing ourselves at three-a-days for rowing. We were so sore, we could barely move, especially me. It was my first season, you know?" She nods when I glance at her, so I continue.

"On Sunday we were stir-crazy. We'd spent the whole week on a constant rotation between our dorm room, the boathouse, and the trainers. Adrian was pissed that we'd essentially wasted our first spring break." I recall the way he bitched about all the girls we could have been banging while we lounged in our dorm, too sore to fully lie down or sit up. "Sunday's practice was light. We were finished by 10:00 AM and Coach said we had the rest of the day to recuperate before classes on Monday. Walking back to our dorm, Adrian wanted to do something stupid, to have some fun. So we drank a couple forties we had stashed under my bed. We got stupidly blitzed since we were freshman." Maura snickers but leans closer, as if she's desperate for the story to continue. "And we went mini-golfing."

"Oh my God. You guys are so lame!"

"I know. We could barely hit the ball straight. I don't think either one of us actually got the ball into the hole at all."

Maura cracks up, swiping a tear from the corner of her eye. "God, I don't think I laughed that hard in a year. So, how did this become a tradition?"

"Just something we kept doing. Hungover mostly."

"That's cool. My friends and I, we go to brunch, but hey, whatever works for you."

"Don't knock it 'til you've tried it," I warn. "Your friends, the three girls you're always with, they're all away this semester, aren't they?"

"Yeah. Lila is in LA. Mia is seriously in love with Rome. And Emma is getting into trouble in D.C. I miss them. It's strange being on campus without them."

"I know what you mean," I say before biting my tongue. "Shit, that came out wrong. I didn't mean, I wasn't comparing Adrian passing to —"

"I know." She stares out the window.

Placing a palm on her forearm, her skin is warm under my touch. I slide my hand down the length of her arm, until I clasp her fingers in mine and squeeze. "I'm sorry."

"It's okay. Really, it's actually nice to talk about him. Everyone is too scared to bring him up in front of me so it's like, no one ever mentions him at all. Even my parents."

"That's tough."

"It's not because they don't miss him or anything like that. It's just too hard for them, you know?" Her gaze is steady, her eyes searing with an intensity that aches.

"I know. Your parents always wanted the best for you and Aid."

"Yeah. And my friends, they never really knew Adrian. Not like you."

I pull into the parking lot of Jimmi's Mini-Golf and park the car. Turning toward Maura, I drop her hand and place my palm on her knee, soaking in the warmth through her jeans, my pinkie grazing a hint of her skin through one of the tears. "Maura, you can talk to me about anything, whenever you want. Adrian included. I know what you mean, even the guys on the team don't really bring him up. It's strange because when people do mention him I'm annoyed but then I'm annoyed when they don't either."

"Exactly! Like, when someone mentions him, I'm pissed that they're bringing him up but when they don't include him in a story, I'm angry that they didn't remember him."

Nodding, I offer a lopsided grin. "Can't win either way."

"No, they can't. Come on, I'm going to school your ass in mini-golf."

13

MAURA

Walking into the lodge of the mini-golf course, I look around and chuckle. Photos of old movie stars and famous athletes plaster the walls. The place is quirky, with fake palm trees, beach chairs, and a salt-water aquarium. Nothing seems to go together and yet it somehow works. I can see why Adrian liked it so much.

"Pick a ball," Zack calls out, gesturing toward a large metal basket with various colored golf balls. He thanks the girl behind the counter for his change and walks up next to me, swiping a ball from the basket. "I'll be green."

"Orange." I pluck an orange ball.

"Let's get started then. Ladies first."

Setting up the ball at the first hole, I grin; I got this. It's an easy shot, no moving windmills or sharp angles. "Care to make a wager on this game, Zack."

"Oh man, you're just like your brother."

"You love it!" The words burst from my mouth and when I glance up at Zack's grin, they feel right.

"I do." He smirks, looking up from the little score card

he's clutching, our names already scrawled in his messy handwriting. "Loser buys lunch."

I point my putter at him. "I like fancy lunches, Huntington."

"That's good, since you'll be buying it."

I turn back to the ball and line myself up, taking a few practice strokes.

Zack chuckles behind me, but I ignore him. Gaging the distance to the hole, I tap the putter against the ball and watch as the orange golf ball rolls before dropping neatly inside the hole.

Zack coughs.

"Fancy lunch isn't fancy without champagne."

14

ZACK

"I kicked your ass."

"Jesus Maura, you don't have to rub it in. I was there."

"Seventy-two to, what was it? A measly fifty-five."

Snorting, I tug on the ends of her hair. "I can't believe you won the free game from the bonus hole. Adrian only ever managed that twice."

"I'm a better athlete than he was."

"I had no idea mini-golf was such a competitive sport. I thought it was something families did for you know, fun."

Maura snickers. "You're so naïve. Must be that farm boy upbringing."

"Shut it, Rodriguez. Your sarcasm is showing again."

Maura grins, rolling her eyes. But this time, it's more playful than irritated.

"You're taking me with you, right?" I ask her as she fans herself with her free game coupon on the walk back to the car.

"I don't know. Can you keep up next time?"

"Maybe if I practice every day."

"You better get on it, then."

"Nah, I'd rather take you to lunch than kick your ass."

She falters a step, shooting me a skeptical look from the corner of her eye. "Good, because I'm going to stuff my face with an amazing, delicious, ridiculously over-priced lunch."

"Where would you like to go?"

"Honestly?"

I nod, thinking the worst. Please don't say *Osteria* or *Fork*.

"Pat's."

"Shut up, you don't really want a cheesesteak for your fancy lunch. Come on, a wager is a wager; I'll take you anywhere."

"I'm serious. I want Pat's."

"Next, you're gonna tell me you add Cheez Whiz."

Maura snorts, bumping her shoulder against my arm. "Who doesn't add Cheez Whiz?"

AFTER ORDERING "TWO WIT" from Pat's, we take our cheesesteaks to go and sit in the front of my Rover. I've parked on Boathouse Row, and we're watching the random shells and sculls pass lazily in front of us. A few teams are out practicing but for the most part, it's a quiet Sunday afternoon on the Schuylkill River.

"How'd you get so good at mini-golf anyway?" I ask Maura, taking a bite of my cheesesteak, an onion slipping back into the silver wrapper.

She shrugs, taking a sip of her Diet Coke. "Wildwood. We would go every summer and every night, Adrian and I were able to choose one thing we wanted to do. On all of my nights, I picked mini-golf. Adrian used to grumble but after a while he started picking mini-golf too." She laughs and it's melodious, like wind chimes. "My poor parents, they probably hated spending every night of their vacation playing mini-golf, but they were good sports about it." She takes a bite of her cheesesteak and groans.

And I swear to God, the sound jolts through me, causing me to think a million thoughts I shouldn't have about Maura. Like the sounds she'd make if I nibbled along the shell of her ear, or had her moving underneath me in bed.

"This is incredible," Maura wipes her mouth with a napkin. "I forgot how much I love Pat's."

"Not Geno's then?" I clear my throat, shifting my weight. Geno's is Pat's biggest competition, and ironically, is located across the street from their establishment.

"Meh. I'm a Pat's loyalist. What's your favorite food? Because, obviously, mine is cheesesteaks."

"Crab cakes."

She bursts out laughing, staring at me.

"What?" I drink my Coke.

"Crab cakes? Are you freaking kidding me?"

"Why is that so funny?"

"Who are you? Some New England blueblood? I thought you were from a square state."

My mouth drops open as I process her words, and then I can't help it. I throw my head back and laugh. "Wait a minute." I gasp, staring at Maura, her eyes dancing with amusement. "You thought that only New Englanders like crab cakes? And what, because I'm from the Midwest I've never had one?"

"Next you're going to tell me you enjoy a cup of clam chowder on a cold evening."

"You are so discriminatory. I'll have you know my mom

makes incredible crab cakes. And they're a staple in the Huntington household."

She holds up a hand. "All right, all right. Don't get so defensive about it. Your answer surprised me, that's all."

I chuckle, tapping my knee against hers. "Yeah okay. What's your favorite movie?" I ask, enjoying this game we've got going between us. I like getting to know her better but even more than that, I like that every time she laughs, her eyes lighten.

"*A Bronx Tale*. Yours?" She takes another bite of her cheesesteak, her tongue darting out to catch a piece of onion in the corner of her mouth. Damn, she's adorable.

"*A Bronx Tale*, huh?" That was Adrian's favorite too.

"What's yours?"

"*Blades of Glory*."

She pauses for a second, her eyes searching my face before she cracks up. "Your favorite food is crab cakes and your favorite movie is *Blades of Glory*? You are a walking contradiction, Huntington! I thought you were going to say something serious like some random documentary on cattle or some shit."

"I've got a lot of layers, Rodriguez. Don't be so judgmental."

"You're right. You're full of surprises." Her smile turns shy as she shakes her head at me. Then it's gone, and she's focusing on her cheesesteak. "Okay, favorite vacation spot?"

"Don't worry, I'm not going to say Disneyworld."

That earns me a snort and an eye roll.

"I like Mexico, for obvious reasons."

"Which are?" Maura swipes my Coke and takes a sip.

"The sun, the beach, the awesome food, and the cheap prices."

"Fair enough. So Mexico?"

"Nah, I love it there. But my favorite city is Boston."

"Boston?"

"You know, you're really bad at hiding your thoughts. What's wrong with Boston?" I toss my balled-up napkin at her, and she moves automatically, catching it midair before it bonks her in the nose.

"Nothing, I guess. I've never been."

"It's an incredible city. I love the history and the old architecture. Some of the churches are in the Gothic style. And then all the buildings from the Georgian period. It's just cool to see so many buildings and structures that predate the U.S., and they're still standing, still being used." I pause, realizing I'm rambling. But Maura's eyes never leave my face. "Plus, they've got awesome crab cakes."

"Naturally. I forgot you're an architecture major."

"Yeah. I always notice things like the building styles and space layouts. You've really never been? Not even on some school trip?"

"Nah, we always went to the Liberty Bell."

"Well then, I'll just have to take you." The words are out of my mouth before I consider them. And it's wrong. I shouldn't say things like that to her. Except, as soon as the words are out there, hanging in the space between us, I realize just how much I want to take Maura to Boston with me.

She titters, taking another sip of my Coke. "My favorite vacation spot, besides the obvious Wildwood, you know, because of the memories…"

I nod, aware that she disregarded my comment about taking her to Boston. And I'm not sure if I'm relieved or pissed that she didn't react.

"…is Niagara Falls."

"American or Canadian side?"

"Canadian. I love the Maid of the Mist."

"Fair, it's a pretty special place."

She continues to tell me about the summer she and Adrian went with their parents to Canada. They were thirteen years old and thought The Falls were so cool. I watch her movements, the way she talks with her hands, her shy smile and feisty eyes. And I realize I could watch her talk all day.

And that I'm having a hell of a lot more fun on this non-date than I've ever had on a real date.

THE FOLLOWING WEEK PASSES QUICKLY, the days stringing together as I fall into a routine. Practice, class, gym, lunch, class, study hall, dinner, Lauren. Every night ends with Lauren's warm body pressed against mine. I welcome the familiarity between us, the easygoing rhythm we effortlessly fall back into.

On Thursday evening, I'm sitting in study hall, working on my thesis proposal when my phone buzzes in my pocket. Pulling it out, I grin as my sister's face and her shock of red hair lights up my screen.

Silencing the call, I walk toward the hallway, shaking my cell at the woman sitting behind the desk. She waves me out of the room, knowing I really do work on school assignments during study hall hours.

"Hey, Nic," I answer as I close the door to study hall behind me.

"Finally. Jesus, you are hard to track down."

"Yeah, yeah. What's going on? I'm in study."

"Right. Like you're really studying that hard during your senior year."

"I'm working on my thesis proposal. How are you doing?"

"Probably better than you. How's your semester been? Why all the avoidance?"

"I'm sorry," I tell her sincerely. "I've been really busy. Classes are tough this semester. You know since I'm not some random arts major with no real classes like some people."

"Political Science has real classes."

"Right."

"You're not too busy to get back together with Lauren."

How does my sister know about me and Lauren?

"Guess you're too busy to check Facebook. Cute pictures from a wine and cheese party." She snickers, and I picture her covering her nose as she snorts. "I love that you went to a wine and cheese party. Who are you and what have you done with my brother?"

"It was lame. You should have seen Marissa. She was wearing one of those—"

"Lily Pulitzer. I know. I saw the pictures. Poor Phillips."

"Tell me about it."

"So, are you guys serious?"

I shrug, rubbing my hand along my face. I need to shave. "Nah, it's chill. You know me and Lauren, it's always laid-back. No drama."

"Mm-hmm."

"What?"

"Does she know that?"

"Know what? Just come out and say it."

"Well, from my elaborate study of the Facebook photos and my strong insight into how your brain works, I'd wager that Lauren definitely thinks it's serious and is ready to pick things up where you left off junior year. She wants to be back in a serious relationship with you, Zack. Not some chill, no drama hookup."

I frown.

"You know I'm right."

Sighing, I pinch the space between my eyebrows.

"I'm always right."

"Yeah, I guess," I mumble.

"Don't string her along, Zack. You need to be honest with her before she starts Pinteresting her dream proposal."

I roll my eyes. "No need to be so dramatic."

"Trust me, I'm not."

"Yeah, well, I'll talk to her. What's new with you?" I change the subject.

"Oh you know, a big fat nothing. I can't wait 'til you come home for Thanksgiving. I'm spending way too much time with Mom and Dad. They're driving me insane. Mom is on a Pinterest binge, and we're making wine cork coasters tomorrow. You know, Lauren would be a good daughter-in-law for her."

"You need to move out and get your own place."

"I know, I really do. I'm just trying to save as much as I can right now. I think I'll move out in the new year. Begin with a bang!"

"That's advisable." My sister is only seventeen months older than me and one grade ahead in school. She graduated college last year with a political science degree and is now studying for the LSATs so she can apply to law school, but in the meantime she really needs to get a life and not spend the weekends flea market shopping with Mom or playing tennis with Dad.

"Yeah. Anyway, I'll let you go. I promised Dad I'd watch Ballers with him."

"You enjoy that."

"Hey, at least he makes the popcorn."

"Tell Mom and Dad I say hey. I'll talk to you later. Thanks for calling, Nic."

"You mean thanks for annoying you."

"If it has to be someone …"

"Gee, thanks. I'll talk to you soon, Zack. Love you."

"Love you too. Bye."

"'Bye."

I end the call and slip my phone back into my pocket.

Is Nicole right?

Am I stringing Lauren along because it's easy and familiar?

And how messed up is it that I'd rather receive a text from Maura then have sex with Lauren?

Yeah, that's pretty fucked.

"Everyone, listen up!" Professor Minela shakes a basket filled with tiny slips of folded-up papers. "In this basket are slips of paper with an emotion or act that you need to display for your final exam. Each of you will choose one paper and showcase a series of photographs that encompass the depth, feelings, and truth of the word you pick. This final is going to count as a quarter of your grade so that's why we're choosing slips so early. You will work on this word, this truth, for the duration of the semester. Ready?"

Silence settles over the class as we nod, aware that this is serious. A quarter of our grade?

Reaching into the basket, I pluck a slip before passing the basket on. Taking a deep breath, I clutch the paper between my fingers. I'm a little nervous to open it. So far, Photography has been my favorite class this semester. We've spent the first few weeks of class focusing on the technical aspects of taking pictures, how to use the camera, managing the different speed settings, the rule of thirds, etc. Starting next month we're going to explore our own creativity through a series of mini-assignments which will lead to the final project.

Please let me have a good topic.

I open the paper.

Broken.

My topic is broken.

Is this a joke?

I should just submit a picture of myself.

Final project: completed.

How the hell am I going to convey broken?

"Everything okay, Maura?" Professor Minela asks.

"Yep. Everything's fine."

"Okay, everyone. You have all chosen your final exam assignment topics. Remember, we are going to lead up to this assignment so by the time you present your finals in December, you should feel confident in the quality of your work. Beginning next week, we will use our class time for each of you to individually work on your inspiration, creativity, and personal visions. I encourage you to take your cameras with you outside of class as well, have some fun playing around with what you can capture over the weekend, hanging with your friends, walking around the city. Use the technical skills we've already learned and remember to enjoy yourselves. I'll see you next week. Have a good weekend." She dismisses us early.

"Maura," she calls as I gather up my belongings.

"Yeah." I stand up straight as Professor Minela walks toward me.

"What topic did you choose?"

I hold up my paper for her to read.

"Ah." She smiles at me, her kind eyes crinkling in the corners. "I know the past few months have been difficult for you, although I can't pretend to understand how you're feeling and coping."

I remain silent.

"Use this." She points to my camera. "Sometimes photography can be healing. It can help you sort out your feelings, even those you don't understand. Sometimes it's helpful to disappear behind a lens for a bit, see the world through a different perspective. And if there's anything I can help you with, well, my door is always open."

"Can I pick a different topic?"

"No, Maura. I think everyone chooses a topic that suits them in one way or another. Just continue to follow the series of assignments and I promise, it will all come together by the end of the semester."

"If you say so."

"I do. Have a good weekend."

"Thanks, Professor. You too." I sling my backpack over my shoulder and walk out of class.

Professor Minela is a nice woman but she's delusional if she thinks I can get my shit together by the end of the semester.

"YOU'RE DOING WHAT?" I ask Emma incredulously on Face-Time as she fiddles with her bangs.

"Do you think I should highlight my hair?"

"Em, focus. Why did you get a waitressing job? How do you even have time for that?"

"I don't know. I could use the extra money. Besides, the restaurant is near Eastern Market. Lots of Capitol Hill people pop over for dinner and the brunch scene is surprisingly fun. Bottomless mimosas."

"Is everything okay? I've never heard you sound so serious about working before."

She waves a hand dismissively, although her mouth is set in a firm line. "Yeah, just want to help Mom and Dad out a bit. You know, there are four of us." She holds up four fingers.

"That makes sense." Emma has a lot of siblings. I guess it would be hard for her parents to send four kids to college, especially since three of them are all attending university this year.

"Yeah. I like it too. The tips are great and it's actually a lot of fun. I meet tons of cool people. And it's only two or three nights a week. I mean, I finish my internship around five, so I may as well do something afterward. Can't party it up every night, you know?"

"Yeah, I know."

"How's practice going?"

"It's okay. Kay is on crack trying to make everything perfect this season but other than that our boat is starting to shape up."

"Kay is always on crack." She rolls her eyes. "She was in my Philosophy class last semester. Total nightmare."

"I bet. What else is going on? Who are you dating these days?"

"No one."

I quirk an eyebrow.

"I know," she whines. "It's so unlike me. But I really have been busy." She holds up a hand, palm open. "Don't get me wrong, I've met guys and all but just no one that I'm pursuing. Yet."

"Well, good for you. I hope when you decide to pursue one, he's worth it."

"Obvi. What about you?"

"Is that a joke?"

"Maura, loads of athletes have time to date. Look at the football team or —"

"Have you heard from Mia or Lila this week?"

"Subtle subject change. No, just emails. Lila's already a smitten kitten. I swear that girl is really overlooking her own advice this semester. She convinces us to make a pact about living life up and then she has a boyfriend within five minutes. Tall, dark, and handsomes just flock to her, don't they?"

"It's really unfair to the rest of us."

"I know."

"He's a football player?"

"A football star, projected NFL draft pick."

"Damn. Lila doesn't mess around. But if anyone could make a guy, even a smoking superstar, fall in love with her in a month, it's Li."

"Truth. Listen, girl, I got to go. My new roomies and I are doing drinks. I seriously have no idea how you're living solo this semester. Don't get too used to the space and silence. We'll all be crowding up your little bubble in January."

"Counting on it, Em." I raise the wine glass I'm sipping on to cheers her. "Enjoy drinks with your friends."

"Why, Maura Rodriguez? Are you drinking on a school night? My God, has living alone changed you."

"It's fine, really. Just taking the edge off after a long day."

"What happened?"

"Don't you have to go?"

"Not if this is juicy gossip."

"It's not. Just tired from practice, and I picked a shitty topic for my Photography final."

Emma wrinkles her nose. "Bleh. School drama is not juicy gossip. You were right. Okay, enjoy your wine. Don't drink the whole bottle." She smirks. "Talk to you soon. Kisses!"

"'Later, Em."

Emma waves, her fingers reaching up to touch her bangs again as I end the call.

Dropping the phone on my desk, I drain the wine bottle into my plastic cup and drink up.

OCTOBER

16

ZACK

"Trying to score a date?" I joke as I walk over to some of the JV crew guys flirting with pretty girls on the quad.

Stevens snickers, whistling through his front teeth. "Nah, man, Steph and I are going strong. But these guys," he gestures to Phebes and Ranell, "they need all the help they can get."

"Seems like it, man. How're your classes this semester?"

"Pretty good. I took a lot of my major core classes this semester so I could load up on electives in the spring. Probably not the smartest decision as I'm already spending way too much time in the library. Time that I could be chilling with Steph." He shakes his head. "Coach is already killing us. You?"

"Yeah, practice has been rough lately."

"Sucks, man. Our boat is slow; we don't have the same power this year. Everyone moved up to varsity and now Coach is trying to pull some of the freshman up. And they are struggling."

"I bet. It's hard coming out of high school, being the best

on your team, to compete at this level and catch up. Not to mention a major blow to the ego."

"Yeah." Stevens looks behind me, tipping his chin upwards. "Hey, there's your girl."

"Hey, baby." Lauren threads her arm through mine, brushing a kiss across my jaw. "Good to see you, Mark. Hey, Joe. Scott."

Scott Ranell smiles at her, blushing. Seriously, bro?

"Hey." I turn to Lauren. "I didn't know you had class now."

"I don't. I wanted to catch you before your class."

"Oh, okay." I nod at the guys. "Later."

"See ya." Stevens lifts a hand in farewell.

"What's up?" I ask Lauren as we walk in the direction of the Architecture building.

She exhales, fiddling with the pendant around her neck. "I was thinking…and I know school just started and stuff, and you'll be busy with rowing but …" She pauses, her eyes flicking up to mine.

"Okay?"

"I think we should get back together," she blurts out, her elbow tightening around mine. "I mean, give us a real shot. What we had was really good, Zack. Why can't we try for that again?"

Nicole was right.

I should have seen this coming.

But a real relationship? I mean, not that I would ever step out on her while we're hooking up anyway but the commitment, the emotional energy, the time that goes into a relationship?

Groan.

Lauren bounces on her toes, vulnerability naked in her features.

Damn it.

I don't want to hurt her again.

But if I'm not honest with her now, it will hurt her so much more down the road. That's one of the important take-aways I've learned from having a sister. I remember the nights Nicole cried her heart out over her high school boyfriend, Spencer. He was a year older than her and promised they could make their relationship work even though he was going away to college and she was still in high school. But as the story goes, he cheated on her one month into the school year. He told her he didn't want to hurt her by breaking up and ruining her senior year. And man, she was devastated.

No, I can't do that to Lauren.

"Listen, Laur, I think we should talk."

She looks down immediately, her fingers gripping her pendant. "Just tell me, Zack."

Jesus, it's like no matter how hard I try to do the right thing, I always end up being the asshole. "I don't think we're on the same page about what this is." I gesture between us. "I was just looking for something casual and maybe the nostalgia, the familiarity between us got to me. I'm sorry if I gave you the wrong impression but I don't think we should try and pick up from junior year. We broke up for a reason and to be honest, my head isn't in the right place to have a relationship."

She sniffles, her hand covering her nose. When she glances up, her eyes are watery and her sadness slams into me. Damn it, I hate when girls cry.

"It's okay, I understand. Thanks for being honest with me, Zack. That's something I always admired about you."

Does she have to make it worse by being sweet and understanding?

"If you need anything …" I trail off. *Don't make empty promises.* "I'm still your friend, Lauren."

"Of course. Well, I'll let you get to class. Bye, Zack."

"Later, Laur."

Way to go, Zack! Cock-blocking yourself.

Why is it always hard to do the right thing?

"DRINK IT!" A girl's voice calls out, followed by a loud roar.

Music blares from the floor below me, the bass bumping. Dropping my head to my desk, I close my eyes. There's no way I'm going to get any homework done at the house. And I'm struggling with the mountain of homework piling up on my desk. It seems like every time I submit one assignment, four more crop up in its place.

Slamming my book shut, I decide if I'm not going to focus on homework, I may as well do something productive. Pulling on some shorts and sneakers, I decide on a run along Boathouse Row.

Grabbing a set of headphones, I unplug my phone and find my keys on the nightstand. Then I'm out the door, squeezing past a flock of beautiful girls in miniskirts with long eyelashes and red Solo cups.

Why can't I just enjoy partying with them instead?

FORGOING THE LAND ROVER, I walk to the boathouse, flipping through my Spotify library until I find a chill mix of acoustic covers that seems to fit my current mood. Turning up the volume, I begin to jog, noting how the sun is starting to dip in the sky, the light blue morphing into purple and pink streaks.

Maybe getting back together with Lauren would have been the right decision. I mean, it's great that things between us are always so easy and generally effortless, right? But is that the type of relationship I want to be in? One that doesn't require that much work? It seems kind of boring. But sometimes boring is nice. I mean the familiarity of it is usually a blessing. No awkward first dates, no limbo period waiting to have sex, no having to meet the parents. We've already been there, done that. And it's not like I actually have the time to commit to a new relationship anyway. Things with Lauren are safe. I could hit her up tonight after my run and we could get together and I wouldn't have to make sure I showered or dress a certain way or impress her at all. There's something to be said for that kind of ease, isn't there?

I wonder if Maura would want a relationship with that type of easy security? No stress or drama to get tangled up in, always knowing where you stand with the other person.

Nah, she'd be bored. It seems like she seeks out the unstable player-types who will just hurt her in the end. The douchebags like the guy from Boathouse Row. A freaking married man.

Stop thinking about Adrian's sister!

She would be a handful to date, to really be with. But at least it would never be boring.

Jesus, man. It's not going to happen. And if you're thinking about Maura, you have no right being with Lauren. So not getting back together was the right thing to do.

Plus, Adrian's sister is off limits.

And then, as if the universe knows I'm obsessing about her, she appears before me. Her silhouette is framed by the setting sun, her long black hair untamed in the breeze. She's standing off to the side of the path, the top of a DSLR camera covering part of her face as she looks through the lens. Muttering under her breath, she changes the settings and looks through the viewfinder again. I stop several feet away, just taking her in, watching her.

And she's unbelievably mesmerizing.

17

MAURA

I jump when he says my name, whirling around so quickly I nearly drop my camera. That would have sucked. This thing is on loan from the school; it's not exactly mine to break. And I don't even want to know what the replacement fee would be.

"Hey." His voice is rough. He's looking at me intently, an orange headband glowing from his blond head.

"Hey," I reply, lowering the camera, arm dangling next to my hip. "What are you doing here?"

"Just getting a run in."

Duh.

"You?" he asks.

I hold up the camera awkwardly. "Practicing for my Photography class."

"That's cool." He steps forward, his blue eyes piercing in their intensity. "What have you got so far?" He takes the camera from my hand and sets the playback mode to begin scrolling through the photos I've snapped.

"It isn't much." I shuffle, torn between grabbing the

camera from his hands and pretending I don't care at all. "Just trying to get a feel for it."

He purses his lips as he considers one of the photos for several seconds. My God, does he have full lips for a guy. Kissable lips. I squeeze my eyes shut tight.

Get it together, Maura. This is Adrian's best friend, you moron. Stop swooning over him. He has a freaking kind-of girlfriend.

"This one has a lot of potential." He holds the camera out to me, showing me the photo I took of a shell out on the water, the Museum of Art rising in the background, the sun shining in a way that shows the shadows of the oars as the rowers slide forward into the catch position.

"Thanks," I say, unsure of what that potential is.

"Yeah, see here," he points to the shadow, "you can eliminate this and bring in more of the colors from the sunset by widening the aperture and slowing down the shutter speed." He changes some of the settings on the camera, before looking through the viewfinder. Snapping a photo, he studies it in playback mode before handing it to me. "See?"

Taking a look at his photograph, I reach out to touch the purple and pink streaks of sunset with my fingertips. "Wow."

"Yeah, it's beautiful this time of day." He nods to the river in front of us. "But this is a tough time to shoot. Dusk is always hard to capture. If you lower your f-stop to 3.5, you'll have a shallower depth of field. That will make it easier to focus on one object, like the shell in the picture, or the museum in the background. I mean, if that's your objective." He takes the camera out of my hands and fiddles with the settings again before snapping another photo. This one shows the museum clearly with the sunset blurry behind it.

"Hey, thanks. That's awesome, Zack."

"You'll have to keep practicing with it. You'll get there."

"How d'ya know so much about photography?"

"My sister Nicole and I took a class at a camp one summer. I really liked it. She really liked the instructor." He grins, as though remembering a funny story. "She tried to be super sophisticated and take photos of all these sensual images. And on the last day, the guy's fiancée shows up to help judge the photos for some contest we were all participating in. Nicole was mortified. It was freaking priceless. Her face was priceless."

"Oh no! How old were you guys?"

"I was sixteen, so she was seventeen. It was the summer before her senior year of high school. Our parents literally didn't know what to do with us for an entire summer, so they signed us up for this lame camp that everyone else stops going to when they're like twelve."

"You guys are really close?"

"Yeah. She's usually a pain in the ass, and she's brutally, painfully honest, but I love her."

"That's important."

Zack chuckles. "Hey, you hungry? I haven't eaten dinner yet, and I could grab a bite."

"You've barely worked up a sweat."

"This run was more to clear my head than to get in a workout. My house is having a party."

"You're such an old man. Avoiding a party, feigning exercise, and wanting to eat at like 6PM."

"Yeah, yeah. You in?"

"Sure, I can eat."

"Okay." Zack smiles, hanging on to my camera as we fall into step alongside each other. "What other classes do you have this semester?"

And as I begin to talk, really talk without thinking about the words coming out of my mouth or pausing to make sure

I'm not giving too much away, I realize how nice it is to just hang out with a friend.

When we arrive at a café, I order a side of fries and a chocolate milkshake.

"I swear Maura, I've never seen a girl eat like you and manage to keep her body so tight."

"It's all the rowing."

"Nah. A lot of those girls are big and bulky, not lean and toned like you. Must be good genes. I've seen Mama Rodriguez, and I gotta tell you..." He trails off, whistling under his breath.

"Ew, stop."

He orders a tuna wrap and bottle of water and pays for both of our meals before I have time to dig out the crumpled bills in the side pocket of my bag.

"You didn't have to do that," I hand him a rumpled up ten-dollar bill.

"Get out of here." He leads me to a corner table by the window, tucked away from the foot line of traffic lining up at the counter. "Cool spot."

"Yeah, I come here a lot. Although I try and order healthier options than the milkshake."

"Special occasion?"

"Nah, just frustrated today."

"Why's that?"

I shrug, sitting on my fingertips and hunching forward. "I miss my friends. And I hate the topic I picked for my Photography final. Just in a crappy mood, I guess."

"What's your topic?"

"Broken." It comes out dejected.

"Damn, you're professor must hate you."

"It was a random choice."

"Then the universe?"

"Quit it."

"What are you thinking of photographing?"

"Oh you know, maybe a crushed-up bottle of pills and voila, broken." It's a bold thing to say, and I know that if my parents overheard me they would be mortified and very upset.

But Zack throws his head back and laughs. "You never say what I think you're going to. That's fucked-up, you know."

I grin back. "I know."

"And yet, we're probably the only two people who would joke about it. Who know that if Aid was here, it'd be a comment he would appreciate. Hell, he'd be the one to say it."

"Are you ever angry with him? For the way it happened … for the decisions he made?"

Zack turns thoughtful, his pensive stare broken only by the arrival of our food. He takes a bite of his wrap, mulling over his thoughts as he chews. Finally, he looks at me and nods. "Yeah. At first, I was pissed as hell. Couldn't understand how he got caught up in that, why he didn't reach out to me. Then I was just angry with myself. How did I not notice he wasn't acting like himself? I mean, I did notice something was off but how did I not see it was drugs? Did I give him a pass because he was my best friend? Because I didn't want to confront him?" He snorts, placing his wrap down. "Fuck, I've lost more sleep over Adrian Rodriguez than any girl in the world, and I know, just know, he would be laughing his ass off at me right now. But man, do I miss him like hell."

Picking up a fry, I dip it into my chocolate milkshake. "Me too. Every single damn day." I hand the fry out to Zack. "Try this, it will make you feel better."

"Are you playing with me? You dip your fries in your milkshake?"

"Just try it you fake blueblood." I hold the milkshake-dripping French fry under his nose.

He narrows his eyes but opens his mouth, and I pop the fry inside. Zack chews for a moment and then groans. "God, that's good. You know, you're as crazy as your brother sometimes."

I grin back, his words warming his heart.

18

MAURA

The ringing of my cell phone cuts through my dream.

Except, it's not a dream, it's a nightmare.

It's the scene of Adrian OD'ing.

Gasping for air, I sit up in bed and flip on my bedside lamp. Damn, I must have taken a nap. Feeling around my duvet for my cell phone, I manage to locate it halfway beneath my pillow.

"Hello?" I croak out without bothering to check the caller ID. I can barely see the screen without my contacts in anyway.

"Maura? Are you sleeping?" Lila's voice comes through the speaker, high-pitched and tight.

"Li? Is everything okay? You sound weird." I run a hand through my knotty hair and settle back against my pillows, wincing as my fingers snag on a large knot at the back of my head.

"Oh God, Maura, it's terrible." She hiccups, and I realize she's been crying for quite some time.

"Lila, what is it? What's happened? Are you okay?"

"It's Cade," she whispers.

"Did you guys break up?"

"No, no, nothing like that," she says quickly. "He's … it's … oh God. He's sick, Maura. Like really sick."

"Okay. Did you take him to the doctor's?"

A strangled sob erupts through the line. "He has cancer. He was just diagnosed. Osteosarcoma."

My torrent of questions freezes in my throat as I try to process Lila's words. Cade is sick; her boyfriend has cancer. Another young person ripped from the earth too soon, another tragic loss.

Stop it.

Cade is still alive.

He's fighting to live.

Not like Adrian; Adrian gave up.

"Oh, Lila." I sigh out on a breath. "Are you okay? How's he handling it?"

"He's … I don't know, he's managing. Coping. He's trying to make me smile and I'm dying inside. I know I can't let him see me fall apart like this, and I need to be strong for him but, but God, Maura, it's cancer. He has to have chemotherapy. And surgery. And I'm freaking out."

I nod in understanding and then remember she can't see me. "But it's okay to freak out. It's a lot to handle and take on. And you've just started dating."

"It's not that," she cuts in. "I'm here for him. I'll do anything he needs me to do. But I just feel so helpless. I don't even know what I'm supposed to do."

"Just be there for him. That's all you can really do now anyway. Support him, distract him, be with him. And don't treat him like there's something wrong with him or like you see him differently now. Everyone is going to do that to him. You need to be the person who still sees him for him. You know?"

"Yeah, you're right. I just, I'm just scared."

"I know."

"Oh wait, that's him clicking in. I got to go. Sorry, Maura, thanks for listening. I'll call you tomorrow, okay?"

"Just take care of your guy. We'll talk soon."

"Thanks." She hangs up and I toss my phone back under my pillow.

Unbidden, the tears come as I think about Adrian. How no one was there to worry for him or be scared on his behalf. How no one even realized he was slipping away, little pieces of him disappearing into nothing. He didn't have a Lila. He didn't have anyone.

And when he died, he was all alone.

Plagued by thoughts and memories of Adrian, I slip out of bed and grab a bottle of red wine from my secret stash. Popping the cork, I pour myself a generous amount and turn on some appropriate emo music. Letting the song wash over me, I pull out an old photo album of Adrian and me as kids.

For weeks after his death, I stared at his face every night.

Our fourth birthday party at Chuck E Cheese.

Riding boogie boards at the beach in Wildwood, NJ.

Adrian dropping his ice cream cone on the boardwalk.

Our eighth-grade graduation.

Prom. Oh God, that prom pose is the worst. And that stupid corsage on my wrist!

Endless rowing regattas.

Jesus, Adrian was larger than life. And now, him being gone has created a massive black hole in my orbit. Each day, instead of getting closer to the sun, I want to slip a little further into the darkness.

And there's only one way I know how to fix that brokenness, to numb that pain, to halt that assault of anger that pumps through my veins like adrenaline.

Slipping out of my dorm, I head to a club down the street.

Sure, I could hit up Hector but sometimes, just when I'm about to forget everything, even he looks at me with concern fringing his brown eyes, making me want to scream.

Tonight, I want anonymity. I need to work out my feelings on a hot guy who wants to use me as much as I need to use him.

The club is shady as hell. Smoke clouds the air even though it's illegal to smoke inside. The stench of stale cigarettes sticks to the walls and clings to my hair the instant I enter. A hulk of a bouncer cards me and stamps a small red circle on the underside of my wrist.

Beelining to the bar, I order a Jack and Coke. Pressing my shoulder blades against the edge of the bar, I scout the talent. One of the guys I spot looks familiar, but I can't place where I know him from. He's tangled up in the embrace of a girl, her fingers laced behind his neck. I shake my head slowly and then the muscled and heavily tattooed arms of a guy in a tight black T-shirt catch my attention.

Done.

Swirling the small black straw in my drink, I push the lime around, and wait for him to look up so I can catch his eye.

When our eyes meet, I smile, slow and seductive. And he takes the bait, meandering toward me with a predatory gleam in his eyes.

"Hey, sweetheart. What are you doing all by yourself at the bar?"

"Waiting for you to join me." I blink once and look down for a beat before meeting his gaze through my double-coat of mascara.

He smiles as if he won the freaking lotto. Flagging down the bartender, he orders a couple shots of tequila.

By my third shot I can barely see straight. His rough hands feel good on my skin, his stubble coarse against my cheek as he leans down and kisses me. I don't even balk as he leads me to the dirty, disgusting bathroom on the second floor. His fingers are lost in my hair, his grip tight on my head as he controls the kiss, the moment, me. I let his huge frame envelop me, encapsulate me, make me disappear for a while and when I resurface, thighs shaking and heart racing, my mind is blissfully numb.

I CAN'T SEE STRAIGHT.

My head pounds, each heartbeat ringing in my eardrums, throbbing in my temples. My throat is dry and scratchy, and my eyes burn in the morning sunlight. Sporting ridiculously large, non-athletic sunglasses and carrying a massive water bottle, I try to nurse my hangover before we push out onto the water.

The oar is heavy in my hands, the boat dragging under my weight as I struggle to get it together. My timing is off, and I catch a series of crabs, my oar practically trailing the shell, stuck in the water, slowing down the entire team.

"Jesus, Maura, focus," our coxswain yells, hitting the side of the boat with her palm.

The noise is jarring.

We set up for some drills and each time I get a small break I'm so relieved I could cry. The water looks cold and shockingly inviting as I sweat, half from exertion, half from alcohol pouring out of my veins. I wish I could fall overboard.

After two hours of a grueling practice, I want to die.

We stow away the shell and prop our oars against the

wall. My teammates guzzle Gatorade and squirt streams of water into their open mouths. I collapse on the ground, lying like a star fish, or a snow angel, or a hungover hot mess on the pavement next to the boathouse door.

"Get up." Kay Hillard's face comes into view, hovering over me.

I squint up at her. Shit, I forgot my sunglasses somewhere.

"Now." Her tone is clipped, her impatience obvious.

"What?" I huff, rolling over and climbing to my feet.

With three inches on me, it feels like I'm being scolded by a nun from my old Catholic school as Kay glares, hands on her hips, frustration in her eyes. "This is the last time I'm going to address this issue, Rodriguez. Clean up your act and pull your shit together. We are months away from starting our season, our senior season. You know, the last one we get?"

I raise an eyebrow, inviting her to continue.

"And I'm not going to risk our reputation or the hard work and commitment the rest of us are giving because you've turned into a bitter, unfocused lush that can't see straight half the time."

A few of the girls standing nearby drop their heads, suddenly fascinated with the straps of their sports bras or the seams of their socks.

If I didn't feel like death, I'd probably be mortified by this public scolding, but I'm too tired to care. Although I am relieved that Coach is locked in his office and not present to witness my dramatic tumble from grace.

"Duly noted, Hillard." I fake salute Kay.

"I'm serious, Maura." She lowers her voice. "I know things have been rough for you since Adrian died. And I know you've worked really hard to get where you are, but I can't jeopardize our entire season on this type of performance and attitude. Stop with the drinking, cut out the drugs, lay off the partying, and get your head on straight. I will not tell you again. If this crap continues, don't think I won't notify the NCAA for drug testing."

My mouth falls open in what I assume is an unattractive gaping hole.

Is she kidding me? The NCAA? Low blow Hillard.

"Don't bother," I scoff. "My name isn't Adrian."

The soft blues and oranges of sunrise streak the sky when I leave the boathouse.

Our practices are increasing in intensity but we're all meeting the challenge. An unspoken agreement has rippled through the Varsity Eight; we have to be number one this season. We all know if we're not, we're letting Adrian down.

And no one wants to be responsible for that, least of all, me.

Adrian is the only reason I'm rowing this season and it seems like my commitment has spilled over to the rest of the guys. We're all pushing ourselves, committed to the season, focused on winning Dad Vail. But Adrian Rodriguez's name is never spoken aloud, as if the mere mention of him will blow the whole season to hell.

My back is sore, and my legs are aching as I walk toward the Land Rover. Clicking the key fob to unlock the doors, I'm about to slide behind the wheel when a familiar Boston Red Sox hat and hot pink shoelaces catch my eye. Maura is running up the trail, an old hat of Adrian's that I bought him on one of my trips to Boston perched on top of her curls. Her eyes are hidden by the brim, but her mouth is set in a line of grim determination. She looks angry and as she draws closer, she increases her pace, her arms pumping furiously.

"Maura!"

"Hey." She walks toward me, raising a hand.

"Running after practice? You're really pushing yourself."

"Trust me, I'm fine. I cut practice today." Her voice is sharp, every trace of the playful Maura I'm getting to know gone.

"You okay?"

She barks out a laugh that makes me cringe. "Yeah. I'm fucking awesome. You?" She looks up at me from under the brim of her hat. Her dark eyes swirl with emotions I can't read, her mouth an angry slant.

What the hell is going on?

"Hey." I step forward, placing my hands on her shoulders and bending so we're eye level. "What's going on?"

She looks away and I detect the moisture collecting in the corners of her eyes. She blinks rapidly, and I hate that she wants to cry, hate even more that she doesn't want to cry in front of me. Without overthinking it, I pull her into my chest and wrap my arms around her, tucking her head under my chin.

Her body stiffens before melting into mine, silent sobs shaking her shoulders. Rubbing my palms up and down her back, I wait until she's ready to talk.

But damn I'll stand here all day if that's what it takes.

20

MAURA

*Z*ack's embrace feels like a forbidden homecoming.

His T-shirt is soft and comforting against my cheek, and I bury my face deeper into his chest. He smells like mint toothpaste, Tide laundry detergent, and the cold wind mixed with the damp sweetness of the river. I wish I could stay nestled here forever.

Kay's words from yesterday morning ping-pong in my mind. And as pissed as I am at her for tossing reality in my face, I'm angrier with myself for spinning out of control.

She thinks I'm on drugs.

Instead of attending practice, I'm out on a run that offers the solitude I crave and the loneliness I detest. Being alone with myself is a relief and a curse.

Taking large gulps of air to steady my breathing and soothe my shattered nerves, I step back. Keeping my eyes trained on my sneakers, I brush the tears from my face hoping Zack doesn't notice, which is stupid since he's not an idiot. And I am literally falling apart in his arms.

He's such a good guy.

What is wrong with me?

How can I receive comfort from him when I'm so damaged?

When Zack looks at me, I swear he sees the real me; he sees all of my ugly faults and disgusting habits and accepts them anyway. It's terrifying.

But not as terrifying that if he knew the whole truth, he would be just as disgusted with me as I am. I want to lose myself so completely in him until I can find myself again. I want to resurface healed, not numb.

"Maura?" His voice is gentle, his hands still cupping my shoulders.

The cold air is a salve on my heated skin as I take a fortifying breath and raise my head to meet his concerned gaze. "Sorry."

He tilts his head to the left, a casual smile playing over his lips. "You want to get breakfast?"

"I could eat."

Zack throws an arm around my shoulders, walking with me around the front of his SUV to the passenger door. Pulling it open, he gestures for me to slip inside. "Then let's go. I know a fancy spot I think you'll like."

Zack keeps up a stream of random chatter as he drives, telling me about the Phillies game he caught the night before with D'Arco, the blondies his mom just sent him in the mail, the upcoming first-date his sister Nicole is dreading on Halloween. I stare out the window, enjoying the sound of his voice, grateful that the conversation doesn't require input from me.

Ten minutes later, we park next to a rundown pancake house. "Very fancy."

"I knew you'd approve." Zack unclicks his seatbelt and turns off the ignition. "Ready?"

I nod, a pang piercing my chest at his thoughtfulness.

Even now, after I literally sobbed snot on his T-shirt, he patiently sits in his SUV in a nearly-empty parking lot at 7:52 AM as I collect myself.

Opening the door, I hop out of the Land Rover, and follow Zack into Pete's Pancakes.

"Morning, guys. Sit wherever," a server calls out as we shuffle inside.

Zack directs us to a corner booth.

"You know, it seems like the only thing we ever do together is eat. I'm not going to cut weight."

"Come on, Rodriguez, you shouldn't be messing around with that shit anyway. You don't row lightweight, do you?"

I shake my head.

"So why would you want to race in a weight class that isn't natural for your body?"

"I'm just saying, I could row lightweight if I wanted to. Not with any thanks to you."

"Ah, I'm not buying that. You should enjoy your life, eat everything in moderation, and love your curves."

"Did you read that on a motivational poster somewhere?"

Zack chuckles, "You're cute when you're sarcastic."

"Only when I'm sarcastic?"

"Fishing for compliments?"

"Not yet."

"Because I'm fine handing them out to you. You'll always be beautiful, Maura. Always."

His words cause my skin to heat, my heart rate to spike, my insides to melt. Warm and gooey and…happy feelings bubble in my chest.

I'm grateful the server chooses this moment to introduce herself and drop off two menus.

After ordering drinks, I flip open the menu but Zack's

hand darts out, closing the menu on top of my fingers. "Do you trust me?"

"I guess so, yes."

"Okay, then don't look. Let's wing it."

"Huh?"

He grins at the server who returns with two steaming mugs of coffee and two waters. "What can I get for you guys?"

"We'll take a short stack of banana nut, a short stack of chocolate chip, a short stack of old fashioned, a short stack of blueberry, and a Belgian waffle with ice cream and strawberries please."

Her pen hovers over the notepad as she eyes Zack to see if he's messing with her. "You sure? That's a lot of food."

"We're eating in moderation."

I snort.

The server cuts me a look, writing down the rest of our order before disappearing into the kitchen.

"Are you crazy? You ordered half the menu! We can't eat all of that."

"I don't know, Rodriguez. You forget I've seen you at family holidays, inhaling your Mom's pasteles —"

"Pasteles are not to be joked about."

Zack places his hand over his heart, his expression solemn. "I'd never do such a thing."

I roll my eyes.

"This way, we can sample a bit of everything," he explains logically.

"You're crazy."

"You're weird."

I laugh.

He grins.

We stare at each other over our coffee mugs for a long

minute before Zack clears his throat. "So …" he leans back in the booth.

Looking down at my hands, my fingers play with the handle of the mug. Immediately, I'm reminded of my mother and how she would sit at the kitchen table in the summer, gripping her coffee mug with no coffee to drink. *Jeez, I'm going off the rails.* "My captain accused me of having a drug issue."

Zack's eyebrows shoot up as he leans forward so fast his chest bumps against the table, coffee sloshing over the rim of his mug. "Why?"

Ah shit. Do I tell him the truth? Do I admit that I'm losing it, drinking too much, going through the motions of my life half-sloshed?

My fingers find the handle of the coffee mug and the gesture demands my honesty.

"I went to practice drunk."

A low whistle escapes his lips before his eyes narrow. Following his line of vision, I note the smudged red ring stamped on the underside of my wrist from the club.

Shit. Licking my finger, I rub it into my skin, trying to erase the evidence.

"Okay, but everyone's done that once or twice. I mean, we practice when it's still practically night. That doesn't hint at a drug problem."

"I've done it more than once or twice."

His face twists in concern, his mouth thinning. "Why?"

I shrug.

Zack's hand inches across the table until it covers mine. "Maura, what's going on?"

"I'm a mess," I admit. "And drinking seems to help when I'm alone and lonely. It makes everything numb and then it's like I can finally breathe." *Oh my God. Why am I telling him this? He's going to think I'm certifiable and never speak to me again.*

But Zack's eyes are patient. The longer they stay trained on my face, the more secrets I let slip out.

"I've been partying a lot lately. And it's been really fun. Sometimes I hate rowing because of how much Adrian loved it. And sometimes I need rowing because I don't want to lose the only part of him I have left. The entire thing is messed up."

Zack nods, his fingers squeezing against my palm until we're holding hands. "I know what you mean. I want us to win this season so badly because if we don't, I feel like I'm letting him down. So we're all pushing ourselves to the extreme. And I'm not sure if any of us really want it that badly or if we just want it for him."

I shudder at his confession, understanding the feeling. The guilt of disappointing Adrian seems worse than disappointing myself.

"But you can't get lost in the bottom of a bottle every time you feel bad." His voice hardens and anger glints in his blue eyes. He leans back, dropping my hand to push his hair away from his forehead. "Jesus, Maura, you start that shit now, it will turn into a habit before you can get a handle on it."

"Maybe I need a better distraction."

"You're supposed to reach out to me, remember?"

"Yeah, but you have your friends and Lauren and —"

"Lauren and I are just friends."

"Really?" I snort, not believing him for a second. "Since when?"

"I squashed it after Phillips' wine and cheese party." Zack scoffs and I'm guessing it has more to do with the theme of the party than with Lauren. "We talked the following week and felt it was best not to start anything up. I mean, we broke up for a reason so …"

"Are you okay?" I ask, desperate to know whose idea it was not to see each other anymore.

"Yeah, Maura, I'm fine."

Our server, with her impeccable timing, returns with a tray laden with pancakes. "Here you go," she sets down plates, "banana nut, chocolate chip, old fashioned, blueberry, and your waffle."

"Thanks," Zack grins, jabbing his fork into a few pancakes, piling them onto a side plate, and passing them to me. After our server leaves, he gives me a hard look. "I'm not going to sit back and watch you hurt yourself, Rodriguez. I messed up with Adrian; I failed him. But, Maura," he blows out a breath, "I'll be damned if I lose you too." His eyes cut me to the core. "I feel like we've already been through this. I'm here; I get what it's like to feel so alone with your thoughts, with old memories, with what-ifs you think you'll go crazy. Swear to me that you'll reach out anytime, any day, whatever you need. You call me. Okay?"

I pour a generous amount of syrup over my pancakes, letting his words, his concern, wash over me. "Promise."

"Alright then, cheers." He clinks his fork against mine. "Let's see how much damage you can do."

21

ZACK

Holed up in the library the next few nights, I'm desperate to finish my assignments and catch up in my classes. Except my thoughts wander after every few paragraphs I read.

Is Maura out right now?

Drinking and partying?

Attending practice drunk is not like the old Maura.

If Adrian was here, he would be ballistic.

But if Adrian was here, would she be lashing out like this?

I won't lose her.

Man, the way she met my gaze when she told me about her captain wanting to drug test her, the open, naked truth shining in her dark eyes almost rendered me speechless. She trusts me so much, and I can't—won't—do anything to mess that up. She needs me. And in a way, I need her too. It's liberating to talk about Adrian with someone who really knew him. I miss connecting with someone on a deeper level, to discuss more than just rowing and classes.

Tossing down my pencil, I've barely made any notes on the diagram I'm supposed to be studying. Frustrated, I run my fingers through my hair, pulling it up on top of my head. Taking a swig from my Starbucks cup, I lean back in my chair. After a few minutes of staring into space, I push away from the table, grab my cell phone and, leaving my books and laptop behind, head into the hallway.

My sister picks up on the third ring. "Fancy hearing from you at this time of night. Shouldn't you be at a party, enjoying your senior year?"

"I wish. I'm in the library."

"Poor thing. All those big words keeping you from going out with the boys?"

"You're such a pain in the ass."

"But, you love me. What's going on?"

I pinch the bridge of my nose. "I don't know. I'm restless, annoyed."

"Maybe you just need to take a break from studying. Call it a night and go home. Your books will still be there tomorrow."

"Yeah."

Silence ensues as I wait for Nicole to infer all the things I'm not saying. We're not twins, but man, sometimes I swear we could be. She reads me better than anyone in the world.

"Hmm, something else is bothering you. And, knowing you, it's a girl. I thought you ended things with Lauren? She changed her Facebook status; in case you were wondering."

"I wasn't, but thanks for the update."

"So what gives? Your head is tangled up in someone else, isn't it?"

"Maybe."

Nicole clucks her tongue. "Can't help you there, little bro. You're fighting this because of Adrian, not because of Lauren. Stop overthinking it. Only then can you see where things will lead with Maura."

Annoyed that Nicole understands my predicament so clearly, I sigh. "Yeah."

"I know you're not going to do what I say anyway, so I look forward to our next conversation about this exact topic. You're torturing yourself over a girl you think you can't have, or don't deserve. What else is new?"

I chuckle. God, I miss my sister sometimes. "Same old. What's new at home?"

"Oh, you know, our house looks like a pumpkin threw up."

I laugh for real, picturing the oversized crates Mom forced Dad to haul out of the attic so she could decorate the house like she did when we were kids, regardless that we're all grown-up now. "Did she carve pumpkins yet?"

"No, that happy occasion is taking place on Friday night. Aunt Marie is bringing Cam over. Mom's so happy he's coming she bought new stencils." Cameron is my nine-year-old cousin.

"Thank God Mom has Cameron to participate in all of her holiday activities."

"Tell me about it. He's the best buffer that ever existed. I'm happy you're coming home for Thanksgiving," she adds, in a very unlike Nicole display of affection.

"Me too. Still going on that date for Halloween?"

"Ugh. We're going to a costume party. How much do you want to bet that it's an epic disaster?"

I snort, imagining my sister hanging out next to the punch bowl. "What are you going to be?"

"Who knows? Mom's Pinteresting ideas."

"Yeah, well, you better find out before you go as a giant bunch of grapes," I tell her, remembering her ninth-grade Halloween party and the horrendous costume Mom made for her.

"Oh God, don't remind me. Mom almost ruined my high school career before it started."

"It won't be that bad. I'm glad you're going out."

"Yeah. I guess. What about you?"

"A party probably. I haven't really thought about it yet. D'Arco wants us all to go as minions. Soooo, that's not happening."

Nicole chuckles. "Remember last year when Adrian made you guys go as Mario and Luigi?"

"Yeah. It was better than his original idea of Adam and Steve." I grin at the memory. I have to tell Maura about that crazy night.

I listen as Nicole rambles on about other happenings at home. The more she talks, the more the annoyance and frustration leaves my body, and I realize I'm done studying tonight.

22

MAURA

I used to love Halloween.

I loved the decorating and the hoarding of chocolate.

I loved the taste of candy corn and the months leading up to the big day, when all Adrian and I would do was discuss our costumes.

I enjoyed tagging along with my mom to the rag shop to buy the necessary materials to create said costumes.

And I adored trick-or-treating, following Adrian and his friends from house to house, block after block, filling my pillowcase with an absurd amount of chocolates and candies.

As I got older, I enjoyed the parties. The creative and hilarious costumes people would dream up. Passing out chocolate to the eager kids who rang our doorbell.

But this year, my heart's not in it. I don't want to go to a Halloween party knowing that Adrian isn't celebrating.

I consider visiting my parents, but Dad informs me he's taking Mom to a party at Tia Jolene's.

Is everyone moving on except me?

But then Valerie Manelli texts me about the Halloween party.

Val: Please come! We haven't hung out in ages.

I stare at the message for a long time, noting the address is walking distance from my dorm.

Val: And don't worry about Kay. She won't be there as she's the only person actually staying dry tonight.

Her words are followed by a series of emojis: laughing face, Halloween pumpkin, red heart, balloon.

Le sigh.

I should go. For starters, it's lame to sit inside and drink alone on Halloween. Even if I did buy myself a massive Mr. Goodbar and a bag of Reese's Peanut Butter Cups. Also, I know Valerie is extending an olive branch after all the crap that went down with Kay and me ditching practice. She's telling me that there are still girls on the team who've got my back, miss me, want to hang out.

So I dig through my closet to see what type of costume I can create on such short notice. Finding one of Lila's ridiculously short plaid skirts and an old-white button-down, I decide to go as a Girl Scout. All I have to do is fashion a sash, add some old rowing pins, and carry around a box of cookies.

Me: On my way.

Pulling on a North Face fleece, I step outside into the cold. The wind immediately whips my hair and stings my cheeks. Above, the branches of trees swing dangerously. I'm shocked to see snowflakes tumbling from the sky. The snow is already sticking to the ground, maybe half an inch in some spots. Each step I take leaves a footprint and I smile to myself. I love the first snowfall of winter. Walking in the direction of the house party, I make a quick stop at a gas station quick mart for a box of cookies and voila, happy Halloween bitches.

THE PLACE IS PACKED by the time I arrive. The party is hosted by a fraternity, although I forget what they're called as I make my way up the front path to the door and note the Greek letters fixed to the front of the house. Whatever.

Pushing inside, I'm assaulted by the smell of cheap beer and vodka, cologne and perfume, weed and cigarettes. The living room is packed with bodies all dressed up: sexy kittens and scary monsters, bloody brides and hot cowboys, a few one-night stands and ridiculous costumes I can't figure out. People are clustered in small groups, talking, dancing around the various pieces of furniture, or off in a side room playing an intense game of flip-cup.

I follow the scent of beer to the kitchen and wait in line at the keg to fill a red Solo cup.

"Oh my God! I'm so happy you came!" A slightly drunk Valerie, aka Tinkerbell, collides with my right side as she throws her arms around me in a crooked hug. "What are you?"

I hold up the cookies with my left hand and place my index, middle, and ring fingers together on my right hand. "A Girl Scout."

"That's awesome! I'm Tinkerbell!"

"I see that."

"Listen, I'm sorry about all the shit Kay said to you. I know now's not the time, but I want you to know that we all don't feel that way."

"Thanks for inviting me."

"Are you kidding me? I'm so happy you came!" She shrieks, throwing her arms around me once more. "Come on, let's get you a drink."

A guy dressed as a farmer pours us two cups of beer and hands them over, winking at me.

"Thanks."

"I'll buy your cookies anytime," he leers.

Ew.

Turning around, I pull Valerie into the living room. We're joined by other girls from the team and as we stand in our own cluster, sipping our drinks and chatting, I loosen up.

And then the front door opens and Zack walks in. Snow falls from his shoulders and hair as he nods a greeting to some of the guys he knows. My mouth falls open and laughter bubbles out when I realize he's dressed as Jimmy MacElroy from *Blades of Glory*. Classic.

Zack looks up and his eyes meet mine, his lips part, and for a moment, time seems to freeze.

All I can do is stare back.

23

ZACK

I approach her slowly, taking in her short skirt, the white button-down she has tied in a knot just above her belly button, the sash of pins crossing in between her breasts. Her dark eyes shine brilliantly and her soft lips curl into a smile at the sight of me. The angry and damaged Maura seems to transform before my eyes into an endearing, almost shy version that has parts of me melting.

"Hi," she says, holding out her Solo cup to tap it against mine. "Happy Halloween."

"Happy Halloween, Maura." I take a swig of my beer.

She snorts appreciatively as she looks me up and down. "I like your costume."

"I thought you might. D'Arco is heartbroken that no one bought into his idea to be minions."

Maura chuckles, low and husky. "You look good in shiny." She continues, turning toward me and pinching the material of my bright green spandex leotard at the wrist.

"Come on now, I look good in everything."

Maura throws her head back and laughs, her long hair skimming the small of her back. Her laugh is uninhibited and genuine. She looks so carefree; I wish I could snap a photo and freeze this moment to always remember her like this.

"What are you doing here anyway?"

"Phillips is friends with some of the guys on your rowing team. One of them is in this frat so I figured I'd tag along."

"I wasn't going to come tonight but Valerie," she nods in the direction of Tinkerbell dropping it low on the dance floor, "invited me, and I don't want to burn any more bridges with my teammates."

"Smart thinking."

She punches me in the arm. "Be nice. I was pissed and venting the other day."

"Oh, trust me, I know."

She laughs again. The sound warms parts of my soul as some of the guilt over destroying her lessens. I wish she could always be this version of herself, not just around me but with everyone. Tonight she reminds me of the old Maura I would catch glimpses of when I went home with Adrian for a holiday or saw her at a crew party. The only thing that's changed is the way she looks at me now, notices me, spends time talking and laughing with me.

Except it's an illusion.

Because if she ever learns the truth about Adrian's death, she'll never look at me again.

I will lose her completely if she discovers that I knew he had an addiction and didn't help him.

That it was my prescription that got him hooked in the first place.

And my pills that killed him in the end.

24

MAURA

"Favorite Halloween candy?"

"Mr. Goodbar."

"What are you, ninety? I didn't even know you could find those anymore."

I grin. "You can find them. They were my mom's favorite when we were kids. What's yours anyway?"

"Nerds."

Swatting at Zack, I say. "You are a nerd."

He grins back, reaching out to twirl his finger around one of my curls. Tugging on my hair, the left side of his mouth lifts in a lopsided grin, Zack opens his mouth when —

I'm jostled by a moving crowd of frat brothers and stumble forward.

Zack's arm wraps around my waist, steadying me and holding me against his chest.

"You okay?" His breath fans over my face, his eyes on my mouth. He swipes his thumb over my bottom lip, and I shudder, nodding.

The air between us shrinks, the scene of the party fading into the background.

"You've got to stop saving me, Huntington."

His eyebrows dip, his eyes questioning.

"I may start to believe in you." I whisper as Marcus calls Zack into the kitchen to shotgun beers.

"Dance with me, girl!" Valerie pulls me away from Zack toward a makeshift dance floor and hustles me between the drunk bodies of a swaying Dracula and a group of Playboy bunnies.

Glancing over my shoulder, Zack's eyes bore into mine, a hunger I recognize burning in their depths. In the next moment, I am swallowed up by the crowd and he disappears from view.

Dancing with Valerie reminds me of old times. I'm transported to previous Halloween bashes, Christmas parties, New Year's Eve countdowns. Mia, Emma, Lila, and I always celebrated the festivities together. Emma and Lila go all out: crazy costumes or themed outfits, wild hair, fun makeup, water bottles filled with vodka, a selfie obsession. Mia and I always hang back a bit, dress more conservatively, avoid drinking except for the occasional glass of wine, tone down our makeup. Ha! If only Emma and Lila could see me now. Hell, if only Mia, with her blushing cheeks and sparkling eyes, could see me now. What would they think?

Valerie stumbles into my shoulder and throws her arms around my neck. "I miss you, Maura! I know you've been having all sorts of fun and wild nights without me this semester, but, really, you should invite me with you sometime! We only get a few months to live it up before the season starts. And now Kay has us all on a short leash."

"I miss you too, Val."

"Let's do some shots!"

"Done!"

We walk over to the makeshift bar, and Val leans forward

to the frat guy playing bartender. He laughs at whatever she says and nods, pouring four shots of vodka.

"Bottoms up!" Val yells, holding her shot up to mine.

"Cheers!" I reply, throwing back the clear liquid that burns my throat and warms my stomach.

"Again!"

"Salud!"

The second shot goes down smoother than the first.

"And now, we dance!"

I giggle, actually freaking giggle, and allow Valerie to lead me back to the dance floor.

She's always been such a good friend.

All of the girls on the team are my friends, have had my back for years.

Have I really drifted too far from them to recognize that they haven't changed at all?

It's me. I'm the one who shut everyone out and then accused them of being too serious. Too committed. Too obsessed with this season.

But now I'm out, shaking my hips and swaying my arms, laughing and colliding with Val. I feel Zack's eyes tracking my every move. And it feels good, it even feels right, to be bonding with an old friend while a guy I desperately want admires me.

He's Adrian's best friend. He doesn't think of you that way.

I have to keep reminding myself, because right now, with alcohol coursing through my veins, a buzz working its way up my spine, and his eyes intent and appreciative, I want to end my night in his arms, consumed by his kiss.

HOURS PASS SLOWLY like days and quickly like seconds. I'm lost to the moment. Of being back with the team, Valerie laughing as she tugs on my arm, Amanda convincing us all more shots are necessary, Amber's hysterical dance moves. The music beats on, the alcohol flows freely, someone announces that the keg is kicked.

And still, we dance.

Costumes transform as makeup is kissed away and bits of fabric shed. Someone orders an insane amount of pizzas, and we descend on the boxes like vultures.

I'm on my second slice, a piece of pepperoni sticking to the roof of my mouth, when I notice that Zack's gone. Disappointment flares in my chest; he didn't even say goodbye.

He doesn't owe you anything, Maura.

He's just a friend. Adrian's friend.

But wouldn't a friend say goodbye before leaving?

I'm chewing my slice, pondering this deep question, when someone bumps into my shoulder.

"Watch it," I turn toward the body now blocking my path. And when I look up, I stare into the unfathomably deep, cerulean blue eyes of Zackary Huntington.

"Hey."

"Hi," I swallow the last bite of my pizza and wipe my greasy hands on Lila's skirt.

"I'm heading out."

"Oh, okay." I try to keep my voice neutral, but even I hear the disappointment that colors my tone.

"How are you getting home?"

"I don't know. Probably walking."

"What? No. You can't walk back to your dorm alone at this time. It's nearly 3:00 AM. Plus, it's practically blizzarding outside."

"Blizzarding?" I raise an eyebrow. "Is that even a word?"

He smirks. "It's snowing really hard."

"I'll be fine." I place my hand on his bicep to assure him. The swell of his muscle, the warmth of his skin through his ridiculous leotard, and the intent of his gaze envelops me; I let my hand linger.

"No way, Rodriguez. I'll make sure you get home. Phillips!" he calls to Marcus over my head. Zack leans down to whisper in my ear. "I'll be right back. Don't go anywhere."

Turning back to my friends, Valerie and Amber are staring at me, their eyes filled with questions.

"Shots?" I ask.

They both cheer and I grin, relieved I've distracted them.

It isn't until later, with Zack hovering nearby, that I realize he's stayed behind even though Phillips left. He's stayed behind to keep an eye on me, to make sure I get home okay, to be here for me.

My heart warms at the thought, and I giggle to myself as I sip on my fourth beer.

Maybe he'll come back to the dorm with me?

Can I convince him to spend the night?

Will he get lost with me for tonight?

Stop Maura! You're friends.

Just friends.

Friends that are playing a stupid and dangerous game.

25

ZACK

The party is still going strong when Marissa calls it a night, dragging Phillips home with her. I'm about to head out with them when I realize that Maura is drunk. Really drunk.

No way am I letting her stay here solo, stumbling home in the dark all alone, or worse: stumbling home under the arm of another guy.

Plus, the snow is picking up and the ground is already covered. It would be tough to maneuver a path home sober, never mind sloshed.

So I stay at the party to keep an eye on her. If it was Lauren, I'd be bored, maybe even annoyed. But I can't tear my eyes away from Maura. I want to memorize every emotion that flits across her face. Carefree, uninhibited, and beautiful, Maura transforms, her edges softening, her anger fading.

I don't want to miss a minute of it.

An hour later, the girls call it a night.

They're all drunk, rowdy balls of energy riding the high of being together. After a rocky start to their season, they're all out, partying and bonding off the river. Everyone except their team captain.

"Don't forget, we don't have practice tomorrow." One of the girls raises her arms in a V for victory.

"Who could ever forget that?" Another girl laughs.

Maura shakes her head, hugging her friends good-bye.

Wrapping my arm around her shoulder, I tuck her into my side for the walk back to her dorm.

"Jesus, it's freaking cold!" Maura exclaims as we step outside, her breath marking the air with steam, like a sound bubble in a cartoon.

I hug her closer, impressed that she's not complaining about hypothermia with her bare legs and fleece. Our footsteps crunch the snow beneath our boots as we navigate the sidewalks.

"We must look ridiculous." She announces, laughing.

"Speak for yourself, Rodriguez. I look pretty incredible in green spandex and a blond wig."

She snorts, quirking an eyebrow.

"And you look hot in that tiny skirt."

She laughs, the sound a thunderclap in the quiet night. Stumbling over tiny mounds of snow, we step in the footsteps of strangers who've crossed the path before us, breathing out white clouds of air. It's almost like being in high school again, the innocence of the moment, oblivious to the weather conditions, walking home with a girl, dressed in hilarious Halloween costumes, hoping she lets me kiss her goodnight at her door.

"I can't believe it snowed this much." Snowflakes thread through her hair, melting along the bridge of her nose.

"This is insane," I agree. "Must be some kind of a record. I don't ever remember it snowing this early."

"Maybe it's a sign."

"Telling us what?"

"That we're going to have a white Christmas."

"It's still October."

"Practically November." She throws back. "Thank you, Zack."

"For what?"

"For being my walking chauffeur." She glances up, her dark eyes shining and burning all at once.

"Anytime."

"Did you have fun tonight?"

"Not as much as you."

She giggles and it's sweet and amused, like a kid staying up past bedtime.

"Are you glad you came to the party?" she tries again.

I nod into the top of her head. "Yeah, it was more fun than I thought it would be."

"Why's that?" Her eyes are dark yet luminous, a sparkle of heat surrounding an island of vulnerability.

Working a swallow, my throat feels like sandpaper.

Because you were there.

Isn't it obvious?

She's drunk, Zack. Don't cross a line.

Damn. If Maura was any other girl, I'd say the line, smooth and easy. But I can't with her. I don't want her to act impulsively on pretty words and feel regret in the morning. But I don't want to shut her down and hurt her feelings either.

Adrian's sister. Adrian's sister. Adrian's sister.

This time, the reminder isn't working.

Because I don't want to look out for Maura like an older brother; that's the last thing I want. Sister and Maura don't even exist in the same sentence since the thoughts I have about her, the things I want to do with her, are anything but brotherly.

They're not even friendly.

"Sorry," she says softly, misinterpreting my silence. "I didn't mean to make you stay out longer than you wanted to."

"You have nothing to be sorry about. You didn't make me do I anything I didn't want to do; I'm glad I stayed." I kiss the crown of her head, letting my lips linger as I inhale the coconut scent of her shampoo.

Maura sighs and snuggles deeper into my side and I wrap my arm tighter around her shoulder. We walk the rest of the way in a peaceful silence, the crunch under our boots the only sound in the dark night.

When we reach her dorm door, nerves zing up and down my spine like I'm fifteen-years-old again, walking Melissa Peters home from the homecoming dance. Standing under the lamppost in front of her house, wanting to kiss her, hesitating if I should, wishing I knew how to take control of the situation. God, I feel like a prepubescent teenager in Maura's presence. It's like all the girls I've ever been with, all the kisses I've stolen, all the experiences I've had to get to this moment have abandoned me and I'm treading on ice: one wrong move, and it's all over.

The last thing I want to do is push this beautiful girl away. So I brush a chaste kiss on her cheek and wish her goodnight outside her dorm door. She smiles the softest, sweetest, most innocent smile I've ever witnessed, and my chest tightens.

Because I'm falling for a girl I can't ever have.

NOVEMBER

26

MAURA

The first snowfall of winter coats the ground on the first of November. The temperature dipped dramatically in the early morning hours, and I wake alone, wrapped in my duvet, a slight headache thrumming behind my eyelids.

Sighing, I sit up slowly and reach for the water bottle and Advil I keep as permanent fixtures on my nightstand. Popping two Advil and draining half the contents of the water bottle, I flop back against my pillows and stretch, recalling the events of last night. The Halloween party, hanging with Valerie and Amber and Amanda, dancing and taking shots, walking home with Zack as snowflakes blanketed the ground before us.

Last night was innocent and fun and a blast from the past that I haven't experienced in a long, long time. Not since before Emma, Lila, and Mia left for the semester. Not since before Adrian died.

It's been eons since I felt that carefree, stupid, blissful fun of being caught up in the moment with friends. Since I gave myself up to the music of the night and danced like no one, and I mean no one, was watching. Since I desperately yearned for a sweet, goodnight kiss.

So far, last night was the only night of the semester I'd describe as epic. Emma and Lila, the center of attention at every party, would be proud of me. But sometimes, sweet and innocent is better than rough and wild.

It was last night.

Stretching again, I'm relieved we don't have practice today. I stand slowly, tugging on a pair of sweats and sliding into slippers before making my way down the hall to the bathroom. After brushing my teeth and combing my hair, I study my reflection in the mirror. Even though I'm exhausted, my cheeks are rosy, my eyes sparkling.

I think I even may be happy.

And the realization that I've been living my life in such despair for so long is almost as shocking as the relief that I feel like myself again. Grinning at my reflection, I twist my hair into a low bun and rifle through the shower caddies girls on my floor keep in the communal bathroom. Borrowing blush, bronzer, and lip gloss, I look like the old me again; not older, sexier, edgier Maura but student-athlete, loyal friend, dependable Maura.

Knowing that I still exist in the lie I've lived since May is a relief.

EARLY IN THE AFTERNOON, I call Valerie to see if she wants to hang out.

Val: Fifteen minutes (snowflake emoji).

Huh?

Val: IMAGE (red cafeteria tray)

Ha!

I laugh out loud, understanding her intent immediately. Racing to dress warmly and find my snow boots from last year, I add several layers of sweaters and socks before I trudge through the snow to the hill overlooking the library.

"Woo! You came!" Amber calls out, waving when she sees me. "I brought you a tray."

"Thanks!" I holler back, the cold stinging my eyes as I walk into the wind to reach my friends. Valerie, Amber, Amanda, and Kay are huddled on top of the hill.

"Hi, Maura," Kay says as I approach the group.

"Hey, Kay. How're you doing?" I smile my thanks to Amber for the tray she hands me.

"Let's do this!" Valerie exclaims, sitting on her tray and sliding down the hill. She picks up speed and hits a bump three-quarters of the way down. Her whooping follows the trajectory of her body as she falls onto the snow-covered ground.

Amber and Amanda follow Valerie down the hill as Kay shifts awkwardly before me. "Look, Maura, I'm sorry about what I said. I'd never declare you to the NCAA for drug testing. I was just pissed off. You're talented, so good at rowing, and our boat needs you. I want you to start pulling your weight and I didn't know how else to get your attention. I shouldn't have said what I did."

"Don't be sorry; you were right. And what you said, it was the wake-up call I needed. I'm sorry I've been such a shitty friend, shitty teammate. But I do want us to have an incredible season. And I want to win Dad Vail. To win every regatta we race in."

She grins, relief shading her expression. "Okay then. We're good."

"We're good."

"Race ya to the bottom!" she yells, tossing out her tray and jumping on top like a surfer, zipping down the hill.

Standing back, I watch Kay fly to the bottom of the hill, note the other girls sitting on their snow trays, rolling snow balls. I've missed this.

I've missed them.

With the cold biting my cheeks and stinging my lips, I sit on my tray, dig my heels into the hill for leverage, and push off.

The wind whips my hair and the cold numbs my cheeks. Even though I can hardly feel my face, I can't stop the laughter that bubbles out of me, relishing the moment of complete freedom and reckless abandon.

This time, in a good way.

FOUR DAYS LATER, dread sinks in, icing my veins in an entirely different way.

I'm late. And I'm never late.

Tapping my fingertips against the toilet paper roll, nausea rolls through my stomach.

Shit. Am I pregnant?

The test offers results five days before a missed period. I'm three days late.

Oh God. How could I let this happen?

I stare at the poster on the back of the metal bathroom door.

Fear has two meanings: Forget everything and run. Face everything and rise.

Jesus, how I want to run. Like a fucking cheetah.

Tearing into the test packet with my teeth, I grip the pregnancy test. The bathroom is quiet save for the spontaneous drip from a leaky faucet. Uncapping the test, I say a silent prayer to the universe that I'm not pregnant. Then I pee for the obligatory five seconds, recap the stick, and lay it faceup.

6:52 PM

Willing myself not to peek, I stare at my phone, urging the seconds to tick by faster.

What if I'm pregnant?

But how? I've always been careful.

Who's the father?

Married man? No, he was too long ago.

Hector? Jesus, I hope not Hector.

Random club guy? What the hell is his name?

6:53 PM

I did this to myself. I deserve to be punished.

But is a baby really a punishment?

Would I keep it?

Could I not keep it?

My baby is not an it!

Oh God, this is the longest three minutes of my life.

6:54 PM

Everything is going to be okay, Maura.

My fingers shake when I pick up the test.

Two bold pink lines stare at me.

I'm pregnant.

…..

My fingers tremble as I sit alone in my dorm room.

It's dark outside, but I haven't bothered to close the blinds. It's just easier to let the darkness seep in, invite it to enter my soul.

Too dramatic?

I'm at a complete loss of what to do here.

My first reaction is to call my friends.

But after no one answers, I decide maybe it's best if I sort out my feelings on this solo. There's no way I can confide in anyone on the team. And my parents may as well have a heart attack that their baby girl is knocked-up out of wedlock. Jeez, I can practically see the tears rolling down my mom's heart-shaped face and sense the disappointment in my dad's eyes.

Nope, I'm on my own on this one. Which isn't that surprising considering I got myself into this mess all by myself. But still.

My hands instinctively cup my lower abdomen. It's still flat, no sign of a little baby growing inside. But I know my baby is there. And already, I love him or her. With a newfound purpose, an energy I haven't felt since before Adrian's death, I stand from my bed.

I need to get serious about my life.

It's not all about you anymore; there's another life to care for.

Grabbing a trash bag from my desk drawer, I toss out all the alcohol and cigarettes in my room. And damn if I'm not ashamed by the quantity. Two bottles of vodka (one Skyy and one Belvedere), one bottle of Jose Cuervo Gold tequila, four bottles of red wine (merlot), and three packs of cigarettes. I'm desperate to be rid of it all and relief clogs my veins as I toss the trash bag down the garbage chute in the hallways.

Once I'm back in my dorm, I make my bed, pick up the discarded and dirty laundry littering the floor, and stack various library books on my desk. Then I sit down, steel my shoulders, take a deep breath and type "pregnancy" into Google.

A new world of information awaits me. As I scroll through an absurd amount of blog posts, tips on handling morning sickness, the best prenatal vitamins, and more, I know I should be panicking.

This is crazy!

I'm twenty-one years old.

I'm not dating anyone.

I don't even have my college degree!

I shouldn't be pregnant. I can't be pregnant.

Yet I am.

And all I feel is a sense of wonder.

.....

My head is clear the next morning when my alarm sounds at 5:00AM.

No dull ache, no dry, red eyes. Wow, I feel good.

Changing into my practice clothes, I run through my old morning routine: make my bed, check my email, and shoulder my practice bag.

I'm about to leave my dorm when nausea coils in my stomach, contracting the muscles.

Saliva pools in my mouth.

I'm going to be sick!

Eyeing the door, I realize I don't want to vomit in my floor's shared bathroom.

Instead, I huddle over the trash bin under my desk just as my stomach heaves and I expel a stream of liquid. My eyes water; tears clinging to my eyelashes. I stay crouched down for several minutes, breathing in and out of my mouth, allowing my heart rate to settle. Standing back up, I rinse out my mouth with mouthwash and spit that into the trash bin too. Then I gather and knot the trash bag, determined to remove that little piece of evidence on my walk to the Erg room, where all of the rowing machines are housed, at the gym.

It's cold outside, an icy chill wrapping me in a hug as I leave my dorm's parking lot and walk to the gym. The cold air settles my nerves and eases the flush from my cheeks. I'm nervous about practice now that I'm pregnant. Is rowing considered extreme exertion? It's something I've been doing regularly since before I learned I was pregnant so it's definitely not a routine change. Still, I don't want to jeopardize my little wonder.

That's how I think about the baby now. A little piece of peace, a little soul of magic and awe. A little girl or guy I'll love more than anyone else in the world.

Maybe I'm delusional.

Maybe this whole thing is crazy?

But I'm already in love with my little love.

27

ZACK

W e have three regattas in November.

We don't take them too seriously—it's still not the regular season—but they are a good opportunity for our boat to hone in on what needs improvement before March. Coach kicks our training up a notch, and we all feel it.

Mid-semester exams are over, and my B average is slipping toward a C.

Closing myself in a library cubicle on Sunday, I spend hours catching up on assignments and readings I've neglected. My thesis proposal was originally rejected on grounds of "lacking creativity," and I plan to submit my new proposal on Tuesday.

Focused on the work before me and determined to bring up my GPA, I ignore the groups of students having snowball fights outside or sipping pumpkin spice lattes at the group tables on the floor below. I need to bring my grades up if I'm going to apply for graduate school. Or get an actual job.

The thought of being a perpetual ranch hand is the motivation I need to get my shit together.

After eight straight in the library, I'm confident about the progress I've made with my courses. Exhaustion settles in my bones as I enter my house, jerking back in surprise.

"What are you doing here?" I ask Lauren, taking in her perch on the edge of the sofa in the living room.

"Hi! I'm so glad you're home. Sorry, I hope you don't mind my popping by unannounced, but I messaged Jeremy and he said you should be home around this time. James let me in." She bounds up, full of energy, and wraps her arms around my stomach in a hug.

Why is she here?

And why is she messaging my friends?

We broke up. Or rather, we never got back together in the first place.

"Uh-huh. I'm really beat tonight. Looking forward to crashing." I tap her back as I ease out of the hug. "Is everything okay?"

"Oh." Disappointment colors her tone before she shakes her head. "Can we talk for a minute? It's important."

"Sure." I nod toward the stairs that lead to my bedroom.

Her footsteps pad behind me on the stair as I try to figure out why she's here after weeks of silence.

What is so important that she needs to discuss it with me in person?

I swear, I'll never understand women.

"So, Laur," I turn to face her but she's right behind me. I grip the doorframe to steady myself before I fall on top of her.

"I have to talk to you," she says, resting her hands on the tops of my shoulders. Her eyes crinkle as she smiles, one hand leaving my shoulder to fiddle with the pendant around her neck. "It's important."

Dropping my duffle bag inside my bedroom door, I take a seat at my desk and gesture for her to have a seat on my bed.

Is she in trouble?

She drops to the end of my bed, her right knee bouncing. Her eyes dart around my room, her fingers still tugging on her necklace.

Why is she so nervous?

"What's up? Are you okay?" I lean toward her, placing my elbows on my knees.

Scooting back onto my bed, she sits cross-legged in the center and picks at a loose thread in my comforter. "I don't want you to freak out, okay?"

She's stalling. What the hell is going on? Was she like this after we broke up last year?

I gesture for her to continue.

She takes a deep breath. "I'm late."

I check my Fitbit for the time. "For what? You didn't have to wait around for me to get back. We can talk about whatever this is another time."

"No, I'm *late*."

What the hell is she talking about?

"I mean my period. I haven't gotten it. I think I may be pregnant."

What. The. Fuck?

"But you're on the pill," I remind her, grasping at freaking straws because I know she's not lying. Lauren Layton never tells lies.

"It's not one hundred percent accurate. Sometimes, these things happen." She stands and walks toward me. Her fingertips squeeze my wrist. And it feels like a fucking vise.

"It's impossible. We've always used a condom."

She shrugs.

Why isn't she freaking out?

Has she already processed this information?

No, it doesn't make sense. We've always been careful.

What are the odds of getting pregnant when you're on the pill AND using condoms?

"When?" I swallow, the word sticking to my throat.

"I should have gotten it two days ago."

"Oh, well maybe it's just stress. I mean, you do tend to get worked up about school and grades and stuff. Mid-semester exams just ended ..."

"No, I think I'm really pregnant." She looks at me and beams. "I know we're not technically together, but, Zack," she kneels before me, "think about it. We'll be amazing parents. And now we'll always be connected."

What the hell is happening?

It doesn't make sense.

Lauren has a plan: graduate, attend medical school, residency at a top tier hospital.

A baby would derail all of her plans.

"How do you feel?" I ask instead, suddenly worried about her mental health.

"Pretty good. I mean, I'm just excited you know?"

Her eyes are bright, her cheeks flushed. She does look excited, elated, as if all her dreams are coming true.

Did she plan this?

A stab of anger tears through me at the thought, but I rein it in. Lauren would never do something like that; she's too sweet, too considerate.

"Don't worry, baby," she coos, and I wince at the endearment. "Everything will be fine. I know this isn't what we planned but we would make a beautiful family together. I just know it."

I stare at her, unease trickling through my veins.

I don't believe her.

THAT NIGHT I BARELY SLEEP.

How the hell could I?

Even though I'm so exhausted I can't think straight, I'm plagued by errant thoughts the entire night. Something is up with Lauren; she didn't seem entirely sane as she gushed about baby onesies and breastfeeding.

I don't think she's pregnant.

Could this be her way for us to get back together?

D'Arco's words about me dodging a bullet roll around my mind.

But what if she is telling the truth? What if she is pregnant with my baby?

Watching the clock tick from 11:00 PM to 3:00 AM is almost as depressing as the thought that I'm going to have to marry Lauren. I shift in bed to stare at my bedroom wall.

It could be worse.

She's smart and sweet.

The poster woman for a faithful wife and devoted mother.

Stuffing my face in my pillow, I squeeze my eyes shut until they burn.

Could I even be a good father?

My dad was amazing. I mean, he was a bit too much with the church-going and ethics preaching, too strict sometimes, but he was always there. He provided for our family; Nicole and I never did without. He taught me how to catch a baseball, throw a football, and fish.

I could do that, right? I could teach a little guy how to bait a hook.

At 4:00 AM I think I doze off. Maybe.

My alarm sounds at 5:00 AM for practice.

Dragging myself from bed, my vision blurs as memories of last night assault me.

Just get to the Erg room. Focus on the workout.

Block everything else out.

I practically run to practice.

28

MAURA

My week passes quickly as I read up on everything I can about pregnancy.

Every morning, I take my prenatal vitamin, forgo my cup of caffeine, and incorporate some gentle yoga poses into my stretching routine.

I drink a lot of water, add extra rest in the form of a midday nap, and have an appointment at Planned Parenthood. Once I have a dating ultrasound, I'll have a better idea of sorting out who the father is.

Please don't let it be Hector.

I haven't told my friends about the pregnancy. I don't know why; I know they won't judge me. At least not too harshly. But I don't have any of the answers to the questions they'll ask: *Who's the father? How far along are you? When are you due? What did your parents say? Are you going to quit crew? Are you going to graduate?*

I have no freaking idea about anything.

Taking it one day at a time, I'm grateful that I don't have to confide in anyone.

Yet.

WALKING from the bus stop to Planned Parenthood, I pause when a familiar-looking girl reaches for the door and ducks inside.

I know her.

Before the door closes, she turns and I see her face.

Lauren Layton.

Zack's ex-girlfriend.

My breath freezes in my diaphragm. Tears prick the corners of my eyes, and I have no idea why.

Is Lauren pregnant?

Why else would she be at Planned Parenthood?

I mean, I'm sure she has health insurance so I can't think of why she would be here if she wasn't pregnant and didn't want her parents to know, like me.

Does Zack know?

A tear leaks out and trails down my cheek. Swiping at it with the back of my glove, I take a deep breath.

Stop crying and pull yourself together.

Maybe it's not Zack's?

Oh God, who am I kidding?

Lauren is completely hung up on Zack. I remember Adrian telling me how she practically stalked him after they broke up last year.

Maybe she's not even pregnant? Maybe she just needs a birth control refill?

Still, I can't go in there. She'll see me and then what will I say? That I'm just there for a birth control refill too? Awkward!

A car horn blasts loudly, and I jump. "Get out of the fucking road!" The driver yells out a cracked window.

Stepping back onto the sidewalk, I walk back to the bus

stop.

THE NEXT AVAILABLE appointment is next week. Sigh. In the meantime, I devote myself to a daily routine so rigid I don't have time to think about anything else. On Friday, I receive a text message from Zack.

Zack: Hey, Maura. How're you doing?

Why is he texting me? Does he want to tell me he's going to be a father?

Me: Hey. Yeah, crazy busy over here. How are you? Are you guys ready for the regatta tomorrow?

Zack: I'm okay. Yeah, hope so. Want to grab breakfast on Sunday?

Zack: Things here have gone to shit, and I could really use some of your smart-ass cynicism.

I snort.

Wait, does that mean he knows about the baby?

Stop speculating!

Me: Sure.

Zack: Meet at Leo's diner at 11:00 AM?

Me: Done. See you Sunday.

No need to read into anything. It's just breakfast between two friends. Two friends who potentially are both on the verge of parenthood.

In college.

But not together.

Nope, nothing weird at all about that.

29

ZACK

Google says women in their first trimester may be emotional as a result of the hormones.

If that's true, then Lauren is definitely pregnant because she's acting like a lunatic. Moody and distant. Elated and excited. Crying and giggling.

I've accepted my role in all of this and know that I can be a loving father to our baby and, if Lauren really is pregnant, a faithful partner to her. I mean, my parents would never accept anything less than a marriage proposal. I will provide for them both and do my best to make sure they have everything they need. But first I want to make sure Lauren really is pregnant, and if she is ... that the baby is mine.

After the Regatta on Saturday morning, I head straight to Lauren's, skipping lunch with the team so that I can talk to her in person. I know she had a blood test at Planned Parenthood this week and should receive the results this morning.

"Laur? It's Zack. Erin let me in," I knock on her bedroom door before pushing it open. She's sitting cross-legged on her bed, an old copy of Cosmopolitan next to her, when I enter. She looks up when I enter, her eyes wide, her face pale.

"Are you okay?"

She hangs her head, the quiet sniffle of tears stretching between us.

"Lauren? What's wrong?" I kneel by her side and take her hand in mine. It's cold.

"Oh, Zack," she says as a torrent of tears gush forth.

Taking her in my arms, she sobs against my shoulder.

Is she pregnant?

She must be pregnant.

Eventually, her tears subside, she takes a deep breath and looks up. Her blue eyes swirl with too many emotions to read. My chest tightens, dread and panic coursing through my veins.

This is it; the moment of truth.

"Planned Parenthood called this morning while you were at the regatta. They got my blood results and I'm not pregnant." Lauren holds up her cell phone. "About fifteen minutes ago, I finally got my period." Tears well up in her eyes again as she falls back into my arms.

Holy shit.

She's not pregnant?

I'm not going to be a father.

Thank God.

Why the hell is Lauren crying?

"Laur? Why are you upset? This is good right? I mean, we're not even in a relationship. Becoming parents at our age is difficult no matter what but trying to balance careers and learning how to co-parent would be tough. You want to go to med school next year," I remind her.

"I just thought that if we were having a baby we would get back together, you know? I miss you, Zack. I've missed you since we first broke up. I tried to be there for you after Adrian died and you just pushed me farther away. I waited for you to come around and then, just when I think we're in a good place, you tell me you don't want to be with anyone." Her eyes fill with tears, the tip of her nose red. "Except you're always with Maura Rodriguez. Are you dating her?"

"What the fuck Lauren? You tried to use a baby to manipulate me to get back together with you? A baby, Lauren!" The edges of my eyesight flicker black. I pinch the bridge of my nose and inhale, trying to calm down. I haven't been this angry ... ever.

Lauren stares at me, her eyes cold, detached, completely indifferent to my anger. *What the hell is wrong with her?* I'm about to press her further when she speaks. And my blood turns to ice.

"I know you killed Adrian. Marissa told me. Marcus suspected Adrian was using your painkiller prescription when he overdosed. It's true, isn't it?" Lauren looks up through her wet lashes, her tone threatening. "You knew all along and never said anything, never tried to help him."

The coldness in her eyes burns with a surge of anger, her face morphing from beautiful to hideous in an instant. "I'll tell her, Zack. If you make Maura your girlfriend, I'll tell her the truth. And she'll hate you for it. Then you'll be all alone, just like me." A ghost of a smile twitches across her mouth, her eyes devoid of the tears she shed moments ago.

Lauren is crazy.

How did I not realize that the sweet and gentle girl I once thought I would marry could harbor such jealousy and hate?

Panic floods my chest at her threat while anger strums through my veins. My hands tremble with emotion but I force myself to keep my face blank.

Don't react.

Don't admit anything.

"Lauren, you need help. Trying to manipulate me by

pretending you're pregnant is sick. Lashing out to hurt Maura because of your own insecurity is insane. You and I will never get back together." I shake my head, a bark erupting from my lungs. It sounds more like a pig dying. "Thank you for just tainting all the good memories I had of us together and reminding me why we have no future together. Take care of yourself," I add, my fists clenched in a rage I refuse to let her see. Then she'll know her words affect me, and I know she's hoping, even praying, for a reaction. Anything to try and control the situation, control my life.

But I'm done.

I've been blind to this side of Lauren for too long. I won't let her threaten me, manipulate me, use me any longer. And I definitely won't let her anywhere near Maura, because the truth would ruin her, and I've already done that once.

———

MAURA'S already sitting in a corner booth when I arrive. Her hair is swept back in a high ponytail, random pieces escaping to frame her face. Sitting with her legs crossed, her right foot beats the air noiselessly. Clad in jeans, a worn pair of boots, and a long-sleeved gray thermal, she looks up as I approach and greets me with a blinding smile.

The clammy coldness that's taken up residence in my chest since my conversation with Lauren thaws. Relief rocks through me, my bad mood fading with Maura's presence. Damn, it's good to see her.

"Hey Rodriguez." I dip to brush a kiss across her cheek before sliding across from her.

"Hey yourself. You come here often?"

"Yeah. What do you think?"

"It's a cool spot. I've never been here before." Her eyes

wander along the walls, decorated with Philly sports team's jerseys and memorabilia. "The signed college Jayden Kelsh jersey is dope." She references an old LaFarge player who now plays in the NBA.

"Yeah. It's a sweet spot. Food's pretty good too."

"Looks it." She eyes the plates of the diners sitting near us. "I'm getting an egg white Spanish omelet and chocolate milk." She snaps her menu closed. "You?"

"Eggs benedict. I always get the same thing." I stack my menu on top of hers. I've never opened it since my first breakfast here with Adrian three years ago. I always order Eggs Benedict. He liked the Spanish omelet. Just like Maura.

"Congrats on the win yesterday." Maura smiles, leaning back into the red vinyl of the booth.

I chuckle but it's dry. I forgot all about our first-place win at yesterday's regatta. I was too concerned about Lauren. And then I was too angry to care about our boat's victory. Thanks. You girls did really well."

"We were okay. Definitely need to improve our start. How's practice been?" she asks, rolling the pepper shaker between her palms.

"You're chatty today. You miss me that much?"

"Don't get a big head, Huntington. My friends are all gone for the semester so it's nice to see a familiar face."

I grin. "Practice is okay. We need to make a few changes after yesterday's regatta too. We're lucky we pulled off first. You guys did great despite your start. How'd it feel?"

"It felt okay but our time isn't nearly as good as it should be. Our captain is driving me crazy with all her new ideas for winter training. Like who the hell wants to do Erg golf?"

I snort, signaling for the server. "Erg golf sucks." Erg golf is a workout on the rowing machines where each "hole" is a short workout that is assigned a certain par. Each member of the team has to complete the eighteen workouts, and then their time is recorded and tallied to declare a winner. It's an intense workout and while it's meant to be fun, it borders along the lines of torture depending on the intensity of the workout. I have a feeling Maura's captain will put the girls through hell.

"Hey, guys. What can I get you this morning?" Our server, a college student, stands at the end of our table, her pen poised above a pad.

We order quickly and our server takes the menus from Maura and turns back to the kitchen.

"Classes going well?" I ask Maura as we wait for our drinks.

"Yeah. I have a lot of electives this semester so it's not too bad. I really like my Photography class, which is unexpected, although I'm struggling with the final assignment. You?"

"Fucking drowning," I admit, rubbing my eyes with the backs of my knuckles. "My senior thesis proposal got rejected, so I had to submit a new topic on Tuesday. I'm hoping this one gets approved. I took on too heavy of a course load this semester with rowing. Probably shouldn't have tangled back up with Lauren in September either."

"I thought you guys were just friends?"

"We are. Were," I clarify. "I feel like a dick talking about her. She's always seemed like such a great girl, you know, sweet and kind and just good."

"Adrian always said so."

"Yeah, well, we broke up for a reason, and I should have remembered that at the beginning of the year. Now it's like I don't even know who she is anymore, and she keeps coming around trying to manipulate me into a relationship." I blow out a deep breath, still twisted up over Lauren's pregnancy bomb. "She's just not in a good place." I clamp down on my tongue. Despite everything Lauren's done, I don't want to talk shit about her, especially not to Maura.

"And, let me guess, you want to talk about it but can't, because you don't want to talk about her?" Maura asks, seeing through my bullshit.

I nod. "Thanks," I say to our server as she places a mug of coffee by my place setting. "Enough about Lauren. What have you been up to?"

She sighs, taking a long sip of her chocolate milk. A weird expression crosses her face, and she takes a few deep breaths before turning her gaze to me again. "Actually, things have been pretty great lately. After Halloween, things between me and the girls on the team are back to normal. Even with Kay."

"Maura, that's awesome." I place my hand over hers. "If you girls are tight again, you'll feel the difference in your boat."

She nods, flipping her palm underneath mine so we're practically holding hands. Her skin is warm and smooth and soft.

Would the rest of her body feel like silk?

"It already does. We're more in sync, shaving our time down right from the start."

"Good. It's tough because people never seem to realize that rowing is a team sport and the connection off the river is just as important as the rhythm on the river."

"I know. It's because it's not a contact sport like football or basketball. Still, it requires one hundred percent commitment from every member in the boat in order to win. And not just being perfectly in sync with the catch and stroke and the timing but mentally too."

"Exactly. It's tough to achieve that if there's conflict between some of the girls."

"Yeah." Maura rakes her teeth over her bottom lip. "Since Adrian passed, I felt like the girls were too focused, too committed. I was annoyed with them all the time for not loosening up and having fun. But really, I think it was me."

I squeeze her hand and don't let go. "Don't stress it. You've had a lot going on. The important thing is you're in the right head space now. You guys will be a contender at Dad Vail for sure."

"That's the plan." Her eyes linger on our joined hands. "I swear, Zack, you're the only one who really gets it."

I furrow my eyebrows, silently begging her to continue.

"I need us to win Dad Vail. For him. This was Adrian's dream. Rowing was always his thing, and I sort of fell into it as a way to be closer to him. I always wanted to do whatever he was doing and it never seemed to bother him. Not like the way other guys complained when their sisters followed them around everywhere." She shakes her head. "At the beginning of the year, I hated it. Rowing I mean. I hated that it was the one thing that still made me feel connected to Aid. It's like the one thing I really enjoyed was now tainted, ruined by memories of him. But lately it's the opposite. I can go out on the river now, meet up with the girls in the Erg room, walk along Boathouse Row, and remember all the good times, be thankful that Aid and I got to share our passion for the same sport. He was crazy about wanting to win Dad Vail. Sometimes I think that's the reason he was taking all the painkillers anyway. He wanted to win, and he would never admit that something was wrong, that maybe he shouldn't have been rowing at all. So now I feel like I have to win for him. And I think you're the only other person who feels the same way." She looks at me and some of the vulnerability that shone in her eyes on Halloween is back but for an entirely different reason.

"I feel the same way. Like I already let him down and this is still something I can do for him, win for him." My voice dips several octaves. I more than let him down but damn if Maura discovers just how much.

"You didn't let him down, Zack. You couldn't have stopped him from taking those pills. I mean, it's not like you gave them to him or anything."

I cringe at her words, the pit of my stomach hollow.

If she knew the truth, she would never speak to me again.

If she knew the truth, I would lose her too.

30

MAURA

Zack's confession that he never should have tangled back up with Lauren shocks me like a bucket of ice water down the back of my shirt.

Side note, Adrian thought that was the best prank.

It's not.

Because drawing on his face with a Sharpie while he slept was clearly the winner in our prank wars.

But I digress.

Zack surprises me for two reasons.

Firstly, I never expected him to confide in me. Whenever we hang out, I have to remind myself that our get-togethers are opportunities to reminisce about Adrian. I can't let my mind run wild with the possibility that Zack would ever be interested in me, even though my heart hopes he is, more so with each interaction.

Secondly, if a woman like Lauren can't hold onto Zack, I am a lost cause. Forever. The end.

The silver lining is that he opened up to me and trusts me in some capacity. The realization that I am still trustworthy warms me from the inside out and eases some of the moral berating I've been giving myself since Halloween.

For a moment, particularly when the taste of chocolate milk almost made me barf on the pepper shaker, I considered telling him I'm pregnant. It's strange because I haven't told anyone. Not Mia, Emma, or Lila. Definitely not my parents.

But something about Zack makes me feel like I can trust him too. Like if he knows the truth, he won't be disappointed in me or pass judgement.

Tomorrow is my appointment at Planned Parenthood. After I have a better understanding of how I'm going to handle everything, I'm going to tell my family.

The only thing I know for sure is no one and nothing can stand between me and my little love. I'm keeping my baby despite what anyone, even my parents, thinks I should do.

THE FIRST PANG wakes me in the middle of the night.

It's sharp, like a stab to my ribs. I gasp, sitting up in bed, clutching a pillow to my abdomen. The space between my legs is wet and sticky and without even looking, I *know*.It's the worst kind of knowing because while a flicker of relief blooms in my chest, a wave of loss so powerful drags me under. Flicking on my bedside lamp, I throw back my comforter and flinch. Blood smears my inner thighs and streaks my sheets.

My baby.

I'm losing my baby.

My abdomen aches with cramps. Pangs of loss haunt my womb and fill me with an emptiness that is crippling. I can't cry. I can't think. I can't breathe. Waves and waves of hurt shudder through my chest. My legs begin to shake.

What do I do?

I have to clean up.

I need to change my sheets.

I have to do something! Anything.

The blood patch on my sheets spreads. Little dots flicker in my peripheral vision. Tiredness weighs down my limbs.

Picking up my phone, I call the only person I know will come.

31

ZACK

"Maura?" I answer my phone, sleep and confusion thick in my voice. "You okay?"

"Zack?" Her voice cracks and its jarring, like sea glass shattering on ice.

"Maura, it's me. Is everything okay?" I sit straight up in bed, instantly awake, mentally assessing where my jacket and sweats are in case she needs me.

"Maura?"

Heavy breathing fills the receiver. She's trying not to cry.

"I need you to come to my dorm. Please."

"What happened? Are you okay?"

"I don't know." She sounds so scared, so timid, so unlike herself. "I need you to come here, Zack. And not tell anyone, okay? Please, I need help." Her voice breaks again.

"I'm on my way. Stay where you are." I stand, pulling on a discarded pair of sweat pants. Grabbing my car keys, I close my bedroom door and practically throw myself over the banister to get out of my house.

The only fortunate thing that happens between my house and Maura's dorm is that a guy in her building is swiping in just as I'm walking up the pathway. Running to catch the door, I stroll in casually after him, hoping security doesn't notice and ask me for ID. The guard never looks up.

I take the stairs two at a time to the second floor, my eyes scanning each door for number sixteen. When I get to her dorm, I rap my knuckles against the door, debating if I should barge right in.

Maura's eyes are wild and unfocused when she opens the door. Reaching out, she clasps my hand, pulls me into her dorm, and locks the door behind me.

"You okay?" My eyes scan her, my hands gripping her shoulders. She doesn't appear to be hurt; at least, there are no visible cuts or bruises showing. But as she mindlessly raises a hand to tuck a curl back into her bun, I notice how her fingers tremble.

Behind her, I spot a thick black trash bag filled with her bedroom sheets and comforter.

"Maura," my voice is deceptively calm, an edge I've never heard before lacing my words like barbed wire, "did someone attack you? You can tell me." I force my eyes back to hers.

Her eyes widen, almost as if she's surprised to see me, as if she forgot she called me.

Tears well up and spill over, tracking her cheeks.

A sob rips through her chest.

She crumbles.

32

MAURA

When I open the door and see Zack, shame slams into me.

Concern is obvious in his blue eyes, tension thick in the bunching of his shoulders, his mouth pressed into a thin line.

What is wrong with me gallivanting around town, sliding under any warm body I can find?

Why did I drink myself into oblivion, when I have people, friends, who care about me?

Having to tell Zack that I was pregnant—and I don't know who the father is—makes me want to curl into a ball and die.

"Maura, did someone attack you?" His eyes unleash a fury so cold, it's frozen tundra. He's talking but I can't hear him over the pounding of my heart in my ears, in my temples, in every fiber of my being. My lower back aches, keeping an excruciating tempo with my pulse. Zack's face grows blurry, the edges of my vision turn black, and suddenly I feel weightless.

Like I'm floating away from all the pain, all the guilt, all the sadness that weighs me down with each inhale.

THE WALLS of the hospital are the color of crushed eggshells, an off-white with tinges of gray. The steady beep of my heartbeat fills the quiet room. I sense someone sitting next to me, off to my right, but my eyelids are too heavy to lift. Instead, I inch my hand over to the right side of my bed. It must be Adrian. He would sit in the quiet with me when I was overwhelmed and needed peace to process my thoughts.

Adrian knows just what I need. Twins are like that, always understanding each other without having to say it out loud.

A warm hand encloses my fingers, squeezing them gently. I breathe out in relief. As long as Adrian is here, it can't be that bad.

Sleep finds me once more.

"YEAH, COACH, EVERYTHING IS FINE." A deep voice breaks through my consciousness. "No, I should be able to make practice tomorrow."

The team. Adrian's team? But that's not Adrian's voice. Still, it's familiar. And comforting.

"I'll confirm later."

Frustration tugs at my memories as I try to match the voice to a face. After several failed attempts, I give up and force my eyelids open. My eyes burn as the light in the room blinds me.

Blinking several times, I turn toward the voice. The muscled back of a tall guy with blond hair held back by an Adidas headband greets me.

"Zack?" I croak out.

What is Adrian's roommate doing here? Did Aid leave to get something to eat?

Zack turns sharply, relief flooding his features as his eyes swell with emotion I don't understand.

"Thanks for understanding." He ends the call and reaches me in two strides, his hand pushing sticky curls away from my forehead. "Maura." He breathes. "God, I'm so happy you're awake. Are you okay? What hurts?"

"What are you doing here? Did you come with Aid? What happened? Are my parents here?"

Zack's face contorts as if I struck him, horror passing over his features. He removes his hand from my hair and grips my forearm. "Maura," his voice is steady even though his eyes are unsure, "what do you remember last?"

Closing my eyes, a jumble of memories and moments mash in my mind.

Adrian's death.

He's gone, really gone, and not just to the cafeteria.

The realization rips through me as freshly as the day of his overdose, causing me to gasp, the heel of my hand pressing into the center of my chest.

The fallout of his death: drinking, partying, lots of sex.

Positive pregnancy test.

Fear, purpose, a spark of happiness.

Pain. Cramping and aching. Bleeding. Calling Zack. Loss.

"I lost my baby."

Zack's kneeling next to my bedside when I drag my face up to meet his. His eyes bleed with an anguish I don't understand. Clasping my fingers in both of his hands, he looks right into my eyes. "I'm so sorry for your loss, baby. But you're okay. You're the strongest, bravest, best woman I know and you're going to be more than okay."

"Do my parents know?"

"No. No one knows except me and you."

My chest burns, a raging inferno. Closing my eyes, I pray for it to consume me, burn me out until I'm nothing except ash.

"It hurts." I gasp, rocking forward.

"Where? Baby, tell me. I'll get the doctor, I'll —"

"No. Don't leave me." Panic surges through my veins as my eyes wildly search for Zack.

"Whatever you need, Maura. Whatever you want, I'm here."

"Please, stay."

"I'm not going anywhere."

"I can't do this by myself."

"You don't have to." Zack shifts until he's beside me in my hospital bed. Gathering me into his arms, he hugs me against his chest. "I've got you. I'm not going anywhere." He murmurs soothing sounds into my hair.

A loss so intense in its yearning fills me up until sleep drags me under.

For a moment, I pray I don't wake up again.

33

ZACK

She's okay. She's alive. She's here.

Pacing the hallway outside of Maura's hospital room, I'm desperate for the doctor to leave so I can be with her again.

Adrenaline runs through my veins, making me jittery. Well, that and caffeine. I'm on my third cup of coffee in eight hours.

I thought I fucking lost her.

All the blood, her lifeless body in my arms, the whites of her eyes that stared without seeing. Calling 911. Emergency surgery.

The hospital waiting room. The same one from nearly nine months ago.

These Rodriguez twins are going to fucking kill me.

The door to Maura's room opens, and I nearly collide with the doctor in my attempt to check on Maura.

"Is she okay?"

Dr. Williams places a hand on my forearm, her touch gentle but firm as she halts my entrance to Maura's room. "She's suffered a loss. Physically, she's going to be just fine. I gave her some painkillers and a sedative to ease the pain. She'll likely be tired and may not have much appetite for the next few days. Emotionally, she needs time to grieve and heal." Her eyes fill with compassion. "I'm truly sorry for your loss. You can see her now."

I open my mouth to tell her that I'm not—wasn't—the father, but the sight of Maura stops me. Lying in her hospital bed, her hair piled on top of her head, her eyes are too large in her face. She's pale, unblinking, and looks like someone took shears to her heart and cut it into a million tiny pieces. "Thank you, Dr. Williams," I say instead, stepping past her and taking the seat next to Maura's bed.

"Maura?"

She glances at me, but I'm not sure if she sees me.

"I'm here, baby. Everything is going to be okay," I lie, hating the uncertainty that fills me as I utter the only words of comfort I can think of.

She closes her eyes then.

Shutting out the world.

Shutting out me.

And I think we're both grateful when sleep claims her.

34

MAURA

"Do you have keys?" Zack's voice breaks through my hazy thoughts as we stop in front of my dorm room.

The hospital discharged me earlier this morning, all intact, minus one fallopian tube. Dr. Williams assured me that I will still be able to conceive children in the future. Although it will be a hell of a lot harder now, it's not impossible. But really, who would want to have a baby with me?

Besides, my little wonder, my little love is gone. And nothing, no one, could ever replace my baby. Brokenness is the state of my heart. Looks like I'm getting an A in Photography.

"Never mind, I got them." Zack pulls my keys out of the overnight bag he packed for me two days ago. My keychain, an oar, dangles and taps against the door as Zack unlocks it and pushes it open for me to enter.

I walk past him, squinting as the bright sunlight streaming through the windows assaults my eyes.

Flopping facedown onto my bare mattress, I bury my face into my pillow.

I should make my bed up with clean sheets.

But I can't.

Every fiber in my being is leaden down with extra weight, a heaviness that permeates my limbs, causing my skin to ache. Exhaustion takes on a new meaning as even the thought of getting up to pee seems insurmountable.

I need sleep. I want to sink into a black whole of oblivion and not wake up until I feel whole again.

So, never.

I pull my duvet sans cover up over my shoulders as sleep creeps behind my eyelids, numbing my senses and inviting me into the sweet darkness.

"Do you need anything?" Zack's weight settles next to me, his palm pressing in the center of my back.

"No," I say into my pillow. It comes out muffled and dejected. God, how I wish people would stop asking me that. Even the cashier at the hospital cafeteria asked me as Zack paid for my coffee this morning. Of course I'm not okay. My entire purpose for living, the one aspect of my life that gave me hope just died.

How could I ever be okay again?

"Maura?" Zack's voice cuts through my thoughts again, his hand rubbing my back. "It's going to be okay."

"Is it?" Can't hide the snarky cynicism there.

"I can't imagine how you feel right now, Maura. Or understand what you're going through. But yes, you are going to be okay. It may not seem that way now but as time passes, you will heal. Maybe not next week or next month but eventually." He leans closer to my ear, his fingers lacing through my hair. "You're the strongest woman I've ever met, Maura Rodriguez. And this too will pass." He kisses the back of my head.

"Please, just leave me."

"Why don't you go take a hot shower? I'll put some clean sheets on your bed. You'll be more comfortable that way."

"Please, Zack. I just want to be alone."

He sighs. "If you need anything at all, call me. Otherwise, I'll be back later to check on you. Get some rest, baby."

Baby. Baby. Baby.

It's only after I hear the click of the door that I allow the tears to come.

They fall for a long, long time.

35

ZACK

"Yo, man, what's the deal with you and Adrian's sister?" Hunt jams half a slice of pizza down his throat. Sitting at the kitchen table, icing his knee, he rifles through a pizza box from last night.

"You know you could heat that up, right?"

"Tastes fine cold. Day-old pizza is the shit."

I pour myself a mug of coffee and pop it into the microwave to heat it up. Resting my back against the counter, I cross my arms over my chest. "What happened to your knee?"

"It's acting up again. Swelling a bit. I've got an appointment with my doctor tomorrow, but I just want to make it through tomorrow morning's practice."

"Make sure you stay on that. Don't let it get out of hand."

"Thanks, Mom. So Maura?"

"Nothing, Hunt, we're just friends."

He snickers. "Yeah right. No guy could just be friends with a girl who looks like her. You tappin' that?"

His words cause a flood of anger to pulse through my

veins. I whip an orange at his head, glaring as it hits him in the left ear.

"Jesus, man, what the hell?" Hunt looks up, placing a hand over his ear.

"Don't talk about her like that. I'm serious."

"Jesus, Huntington. What the hell has gotten into you? You never had a problem before talking about how great Lauren is in the sack and she was your fucking girlfriend."

Striding over to Hunt in three steps, I lean down so we're eye level. "Maura isn't Lauren. I swear to God, Jeremy, another word about her better not come out of your mouth."

His eyes widen as he realizes I'm serious. Holding his hands up in surrender, he mutters, "Okay, man, relax."

The timer on the microwave dings, and I move away from Hunt, still pissed at him for talking about Maura like that and pissed at myself for reacting like a deranged lunatic. Taking my coffee from the microwave, I leave the kitchen.

Why the hell am I about to knock my friend's teeth down his throat for asking if I'm hooking up with Maura?

Of course the guys have noticed that Maura and I are kicking it lately.

Are my feelings for her that obvious?

Clenching my hands into fists, I sit on the edge of my bed. Maura's face appears in my mind, pale and scared and devastated. Jesus, she broke my heart at the hospital. The tears she cried, the anguished sobs that ripped from her throat when she thought she was alone, the hiccups that wouldn't settle for hours. I stood outside her door and wished that I could stride inside, gather her up, and let her pain seep into my skin. I wish I could absorb all of it for her so she doesn't have to battle so many emotions at once.

But I knew she would be horrified. No matter how many times I reach out to her, regardless of the connection between us, Maura has a hard time letting anyone in. She's used to suffering alone, to bearing the burden of Adrian's passing by herself, to checking her emotions and pasting a smile on her face because it's easier that way. Easier for everyone except her.

And God, I hate that some guy, some random asshole who doesn't know her or care about her the way I do, put a baby inside her belly. I don't care how that makes me sound. Learning that Maura was pregnant hurt; it sliced through my chest and burned my stomach. *She deserves more. Better.*

She deserves it all.

Sitting on the corner of my bed, I sigh, letting my head fall into my open palms, my elbows propped up on my knees.

How am I supposed to help her heal?

How do I best support her?

Damn, I need to sort out my shit.

I need to make Maura understand that I'm not going anywhere, that I'm always here for her.

And not because Adrian was my best friend.

But because I care about her.

Because I want her in my life.

Because my feelings for her have nothing to do with her twin and everything to do with her, and how I feel when I'm with her.

"Hey, dude." A double knock on my door in quick succession is followed by Bilson's head appearing around the door frame. "You good?"

"I snapped at Hunt."

"I heard." James steps inside my bedroom and closes the door behind him, leaning against it and crossing his arms over his chest. "What's the deal?"

"Fuck." I blow out, pinching the bridge of my nose. "My head's all tangled up." How can I explain the emotional stress of the past few weeks without giving everything away? Lauren's baby scare followed by Maura's health scare has me dangling over the edge, but I don't want to betray either of their trust by confiding in Bilson, even though he's a steel vault.

"Look," Bilson spins around in my desk chair and props his feet on my bed. "I don't know what's going on lately. But we can all tell that you've been really stressed out. I know you've got a tough course load and practices have been intense but it's more than that. And I know you're not going to tell me what it is."

I dip my chin, waiting for him to continue.

"Zack, you're a good dude. A solid guy. So I'm going to tell it to you straight from an outsider's perspective, yeah?"

"Okay."

"The way you're acting toward Maura Rodriguez," he blows out a low whistle, "you're not thinking straight. She's got you all twisted up. You're defensive of your relationship with her and pissed if anyone mentions her name. Dude, you're into her so hard, but you won't admit it, can't admit it, even to yourself, because you think you're betraying Adrian. But we can all see it. Zack, you want Maura. And you're fighting it because of Adrian and because Maura's not in the right place to do the whole relationship thing right now."

Who is he, Dr. Phil?

"But you need to realize that as protective as Adrian was over his sister, he was your best friend. And you knew him. Do you really think he would object to you dating, really caring about Maura? Do you think he would rather see her with some of the douchebags she's been rolling with lately?"

I raise my eyebrows at him.

"Phillips told me about the guy she was with at the Rittenhouse, and I saw her at a club about a month ago. The guy she was with looked like the Hulk and I don't think she even caught his name before disappearing with him."

I cringe, my hands clenching into fists. *One of them fathered her baby and doesn't even know it.*

"You think Adrian would rather have one of those guys tangle up with her? I don't. I think he would much rather it was you. As long as he knew you were for real. And you are, dude. You're more for real about Maura than you ever were about any girl, including Lauren. And at one point, you freaking thought she was the one. And as for Maura not being in the right head space for a real relationship, so what? There's not an expiration date. Give her time, be there for her, and when she's ready, she'll let you know."

"You're right." I admit, my shoulders relaxing as some of the tension I've been carrying around subsides. I've been so focused on not crossing any lines with Maura because of my friendship with Adrian that I've made a mess of things between us.

"I know I am, bro. One more thing."

"What?"

"Before you do anything, go home and enjoy Thanksgiving with your family. After a few rounds with Nicole, you'll come back with a fresh perspective and in a better mood." He snorts. "Your sister really knows how to push your buttons."

"Damn." I grip the back of my neck. "You have no idea, Bilson."

"Happy Thanksgiving, Huntington. I'm heading out after practice tomorrow. When you get back, settle this shit."

"Yeah, I will. Thanks, James."

He stands and opens my bedroom door. "By the way, the house is doing our pre-Thanksgiving tradition tonight. 7:00 PM."

"I wasn't sure if everyone was still up for that."

"Can't let all of our traditions go. Adrian would want us to keep Thanksgiving."

"Yeah, he would. I'll be there."

"Good."

I listen to his footsteps thump back down the stairs.

ME: *Hey, how you feeling tonight?*

Me: *Do you need anything?*

My messages to Maura remain unanswered but I know she's not just avoiding me, she's avoiding the world. So I give her space, give her time, because when I settle things between us and make her understand all the ways I want to commit to her, to us, she won't be hiding from me.

Packing a bag of clothes and some text books for Thanksgiving break, I walk into the kitchen.

"Something smells good."

"Hunt ordered a turkey wrapped in bacon." D'Arco explains, tossing me a beer.

I catch it and pop the tab, taking a long gulp. "You did good, Jeremy. About before, I —"

"I get it, man. Don't stress it. Let's enjoy dinner."

Nodding, I slide into a chair at the table.

"This is a sick spread." Bilson piles his plate with turkey, mashed potatoes, and mac and cheese. "Dude, did your mom send the apple pie?"

D'Arco nods. "Hell yeah. She knows it's my favorite and I'm her favorite kid so…"

"We all benefit." I grin, taking another swig of beer.

"Exactly." D'Arco raises his beer. "Happy Thanksgiving."

"Happy Thanksgiving." We echo, sitting around the table.

For hours, we joke and reminisce, share stories of Adrian and joke about stupid pranks. And it feels good, like old times.

Before Adrian died.

Before I learned to live with a pit of guilt in the center of my stomach.

Before I fell for Maura Rodriguez.

36

MAURA

M y first Thanksgiving without Adrian is hard.
Really, really hard.

After months of zapped energy and blank eyes, Mom declines an invitation to my Tio and Tia's house and insists on cooking our usual Thanksgiving dinner. It was Adrian's favorite holiday and she wants to carry on the tradition for him.

So Mom, Dad, and I sit around the dining table and try to regain normalcy. We discuss my Photography class and the Varsity Eight. We smile at Dad's jokes and comment on the new spice rack Mom purchased.

We avoid glancing at Adrian's empty chair.

And survive our first Thanksgiving without the person we were all most thankful for.

After dinner, I think we're all relieved to escape to the noisiness of Tio Jorge and Tia Ana's home. Their home provides the perfect distraction. My cousins entertain me with the latest occurrences in their lives: boyfriends and girl-friends, football season, college applications. Tia Ana and Tia Jolene captivate me with a hysterical recounting of how my cousin Jose tried to fix his unibrow and ended up shaving off most of his eyebrows. Tio Jorge slips me a twenty-dollar bill for "beer money."

During spontaneous moments, I find myself enjoying the company, the conversation, the holiday. And then I remember that Adrian is gone and so is my baby, and I feel devastatingly guilty.

(4:48PM) *Zack: Happy Thanksgiving, Maura.*

(6:03PM) *Zack: Sleeping off that tryptophan?*

(7:36PM) *Zack: I miss you.*

(9:18PM) *Zack: If you want to talk, I'm here. If not, I'm still here.*

Zack is my one bright spot in all of the destruction I caused in my life. Each time my

phone chimes with a new message, I hope it's him. And when it is, I can't stop the flicker of a smile that ghosts my lips.

I'm not ready to talk to him.

I'm not ready to reach out and have the conversation we've been skirting around for weeks.

But his messages warm my heart.

And I can't help but miss him.

ON FRIDAY, I take the train up to New York to visit Lila.

"Thank God you're here." Lila pulls me into a hug, the strawberry scent of her hair enveloping me.

"I missed you, Li."

"I need you, Maura." She pulls back, her eyes wounded and guarded and searching. She's a muted version of herself, pale instead of vibrant, her eyes dull instead of dancing. A few weeks ago, Lila was sexually assaulted and as I tug her closer for another hug, I know that she's lost and struggling. That she feels stuck and doesn't know how to move forward.

"It gets easier." I murmur. "Maybe not better. And not only because of passing time. But at some point, you decide to take a step and then, things are more manageable."

"You're the only person whose been honest with me."

"That's because I've been where you're at. Not the same circumstances and I'm not trying to equate the two. But I've been lost, Li. Most days, I still am."

"Thanks for coming."

"Always."

Even though she doesn't say it, I know that on top of everything she's dealing with, she's nursing a shattered heart. I guess in a way I am too. Although, a boy broke her heart while I'm solely responsible for my own heartache. Either way, neither of us is much company, but I feel better being around her.

"Come on, let's make some popcorn and watch a movie or something."

Making a bag of popcorn and pouring two Diet Cokes, I follow Lila into the living room. We sit on the couch and I grab a handful of the popcorn she offers. We're chatting about random movies and bits of gossip when Lila's mom takes a seat on the armchair and flips the channel to ESPN.

And there, speaking out against sexual assault on college campuses, is Cade. Lila's Cade. Defending her, protecting her, loving her.

"Holy shit." I chew my mouthful of popcorn, my eyes glued to Cade's face on the television. "He loves you."

Moments later, Lila's mom echoes my thoughts.

I take Lila's hand in mine and when I glance over at her, her eyes are brimming with tears and hope.

I've never been so grateful to someone I've never met,

but Cade Wilkins is truly a special man. And I'm beyond thankful for his presence in my friend's life. "What are you going to do?"

But she's too focused on Cade to respond.

And besides, I already know the answer.

LATER THAT NIGHT I twist my hair up into a bun on top of my head to take a quick shower. Shedding my clothes, I study my reflection in the mirror. Turning to the side, I note my profile. My belly is still flat. No sign of my pregnancy, nothing that shows just weeks ago a little miracle grew there.

It's like nothing ever happened.

How do you overcome something that you can't see?

How can anyone understand a loss that doesn't leave visible scars?

Does Lila feel the same sense of devastation that over-whelms me?

To a passerby, I look normal. Yet inside, my heart is broken, my spirit shattered.

Will I ever feel whole again?

Or will I forever be shrouded in loss? It has scored my heart, marked my soul, and I fear I will never feel like myself again.

ON SUNDAY, I leave Lila's house and take the train back to Philadelphia.

"You're going to be okay, Maura." She hugs me goodbye, holding tight for an extra squeeze.

"So are you."

"I know." She tries to smile. "Whoever thought we would be this far out of our comfort zones?"

I snort. "Stupid pact. It was your dumb idea."

"I know." Lila smirks and this time, some of her spunk is evident. " But, I'm glad we did the pact. Regardless of everything, I've learned a lot this semester."

I consider her words. No one told me to become a lush and sleep around to push past my comfort zone; I made those decisions all on my own. Still, I cup my abdomen protectively, I'd never give up knowing what it was like to have had my little wonder, even for such a short time. "Me too."

"Don't be such a stranger. Call from time to time, okay?"

"I will."

"Take care of yourself."

"You too."

She turns around to help me with my bag.

"Li?"

"Hmm."

I wait until she looks up, makes eye contact with me. "You deserve something good. Someone like Cade. Don't let him go."

"So do you, Maura. When the right guy comes along, don't shut him out."

37

ZACK

Thanksgiving in the Huntington household is always over the top.

This year is no different.

Mom decorated in autumn colors; a wreath made of leaves, pinecones, and gold ribbon on the front door and bouquets of dahlias, mums, and Queen Anne's lace sprout from twine-covered mason jars.

I know you're wondering how I know so much about flowers. But, after years of being forced to decorate and create the floral arrangements, I'm on top of my game.

"Straight out of Pinterest." My sister winks at me as she places a chocolate turkey next to each place setting in the dining room.

"Mom's happy."

She chuckles. "Mom's always happy."

It's the truth. Nicole and I are lucky when it comes to our parents. While most of my friends and teammates dread going home for the long winter break or summer vacations, Nicole and I always enjoyed reuniting back at Mom and Dad's. Our mom never missed a football game, gymnastics meet, or school bake sale. She always created our homemade Halloween costumes and birthday cakes. Dinners were always a time to gather, chat, and reflect.

Our dad worked hard, but when he walked through the front door at 7:00 PM, his eyes lit up at the sight of Mom turning a wooden spoon in a big pot on the stove or pressing one of his shirts on the iron. He worships her. And she idolizes him. And although our household was one delineated on strict gender roles and old-fashioned notions, our parents have an incredibly loving marriage, and Nicole and I benefitted from a stable and nurturing upbringing.

The holidays always reinforce how fortunate I am.

"Grandma Chloe, sit at the head of the table." Dad grins, carving the turkey.

"Oh, you don't have to do that."

"Come on, Grandma, we all know you're dying to say grace." My cousin Emery calls out, lifting her fork.

"Well," Grandma grins, slipping into the seat and presiding over the dining table like the family matriarch she is, "if you insist."

Mom winks and I grin, slipping into my chair.

We say grace, raise our wine glasses in a toast, and descend like vultures on the plates piled high with Thanksgiving sides.

The dining room echoes with conversation until the tryptophan kicks in.

"Nap time?" One of my cousins asks and all the cousins stand, gathering pillows and quilts and collapsing in a haphazard cluster in front of the fireplace to snooze, football on the television.

"I love this tradition." Nicole murmurs, closing her eyes.

"I love napping." Emery replies, fluffing her pillow next to mine. "No Lauren this year?"

"No," I say, not bothering to elaborate.

"I heard you guys were back together."

"We're not. We had a brief moment in September but never got back together."

"That's not your Facebook status."

"I don't have a Facebook status."

She snickers. "You should check Lauren's updates then. Her status is: It's Complicated. She was posting as if you guys were already engaged. Although, you're right; her posts have died down a bit. Still, we were all expecting to see her. Well, Cam was just hoping she'd be here."

"Ah, to be nine years old and in love."

"Hey!" Cameron sits on me, "I'm nine and three-quarters now."

"My bad big man," I roll him off of me and he nestles into the space beside me, hogging my pillow.

"It's not like that between Lauren and me." I say to Emery. "It never was."

Nicole snorts on my other side, and I elbow her in the ribs.

"You should make sure Lauren knows that," Emery pulls a quilt around her shoulders and turns on her side.

Glancing at Nicole, I raise my eyebrows. *What is that about?*

Nicole's eyes widen in response. *Emery and Scott broke up. She's projecting.*

I nod in understanding.

Nicole stifles a laugh by pretending to yawn and turns away from me, snuggling into her pillow.

Nestled between my sister and Emery, with Cam's stinky feet kicking me in the ribs, I close my eyes and try not to think about Maura. I try to think of nothing and just relax. Little by little, the stiffness in my back subsides, the soreness in my shoulders eases, and I start to drift. Maybe it's because for a moment I'm reliving my childhood. Maybe it's because the beer has gone straight to my head. Or maybe it's because being with family always manages to put everything in perspective. But when I do fall asleep, I'm completely out.

Later, Nicole tells me I snored.

"War!" Nicole announces, flipping over her next card. Nine of hearts.

We both count out three cards facedown and flip over a fourth. "You win," I note her King of Spades. Pushing all the cards in her direction, she stacks them neatly and adds them to the end of her pile.

"So," she sips her coffee spiked with Bailey's, "what gives? You were quiet today. And you're never quiet."

I shrug, glancing around the kitchen. Hours ago this room was buzzing with chatter, filled with delicious aromas, swarming with people. It was also a massive mess as piled dishes littered countertops and half-empty beer bottles lined the windowsill over the sink. Now, it's quiet and calm and clean with just a hint of the organic lemon cleaner Mom uses hanging in the air. I've always loved Thanksgiving, loved the food most but also the company. My family is big and loud and crazy. But they're mine. And today I enjoyed just watching the interactions between everyone. "It was a nice day. Good to be home.

"Right. So what happened with Lauren?"

"Wow, no lead-up there. Just going in straight for the kill, huh?" I swipe the two cards as I win the round.

"I've never been known for my subtlety."

"That may be the most truthful thing you've ever said."

"Please, I'm always truthful. So?"

"I ended it at the start of October after we talked. You were right, and I told her I didn't want to get back together, that we broke up for a reason, that I thought we were just doing casual."

"Casual is a word Lauren never understood. What happened? You should really check your social media more often. Or just delete it if you're going to be the weirdest college kid on Earth and not stalk people on it."

"This is why I hate social media."

"Well, Lauren loves it and she posted all through October like something was going on between you guys."

"She's bizarre sometimes. You know D'Arco told me after we broke up last year she would wait around the house looking for me, send the guys messages to see where I was."

Nicole raises her eyebrows but doesn't look surprised.

"What?" I ask her.

"Nothing. I mean, I can see that."

"You can? Is it just me that never realized she had stalker tendencies?"

"Probably. You always see the best in everyone and over-look their shortcomings."

"Anyway," I flip over another card, "she thought she was pregnant."

Nicole chokes on her coffee. "What?" Her eyes widen, gold flecks shimmering in pools of brown as she tosses her red hair over her shoulder. "It was a scare?"

"I think so. I'm not sure. She was elated about the whole thing. Kept going on about how we would be amazing parents and make a beautiful family. It's like she really wanted us to be having a baby. And when she found out she wasn't preg-nant, she started throwing Maura in my face. Telling me that —" I cut myself off, not wanting to tell Nicole that Adrian died after swiping my old prescriptions. "Telling me that she would tell Maura all sorts of shit if I asked her out."

"Jesus." Nicole slaps her pile of cards down, ignoring my Queen of Diamonds in the middle of the table.

"I know."

"Are you going to ask Maura out?"

"I don't know what the hell I'm doing. I want to. I'm just not sure now is the right time."

Nicole tilts her head at me. "Why?"

"Timing's off."

"Timing is never going to be perfect with something like that."

"I guess." I take a swig of the beer next to me. It's lukewarm.

"When did you guys start hanging out?"

"Since school started. I ran into her and ..." I trail off. Neither of us is even playing cards anymore.

"And ...?"

"We hang out from time to time. Talk about Aid."

"But you like her. Really like her," Nicole presses, observant as ever. No one has ever been able to read me like my sister.

I nod, looking up at her. "That's fucked, right?"

"Not that you have feelings for her, no. It's honest."

"I just don't know what Adrian would say about it all."

"Are you kidding me? If it was anyone else, he would probably want to shoot them. But I think he would be excited about getting you for a brother-in-law."

"Well, my nonexistent relationship with Maura just escalated. Thanks, Nic."

"That's what sisters are for." She adds more Baileys to her coffee. "Want to get drunk with me?"

"Fuck yeah. I think I need to get drunk."

"You can start figuring out how you're going to ask Maura out tomorrow. You know, when you're hungover."

See? Sometimes coming home is all the perspective a guy needs.

Nicole slides a shot glass across the table at me. Shaking my head, I walk over to our parents' liquor cabinet and grab a bottle of vodka. Uncapping the bottle, I pour out two shots.

"To annoying, nosy sisters." I raise my glass.

"To emotionally-challenged little brothers."

We both chuckle.

And then we drink.

38

MAURA

"What are you doing here?" I ask Lauren as I walk up to my dorm building, shouldering my weekender bag.

"I was waiting for you."

"Why?" I drop my bag on the ground and face her.

She regards me cautiously, fiddling with the pendant around her neck. Her hair is swept into a high ponytail, her makeup perfect. Lauren is always sophisticated, poised, and an Instagram photoshoot waiting to happen. It's beyond irritating.

"I have to tell you something."

"Listen, if this is about Zack, I think you should talk to —"

"It's about Adrian."

"Adrian?" Surprise rocks my system, my chest tightening. And I know in my heart of hearts, down to the density of my bones, that whatever Lauren says next is going to be bad. Devastatingly so. "What about Adrian?"

"His overdose, it isn't what you think."

"What are you talking about?" I step forward but Lauren holds her ground, a tiny smile flickering over her lips.

"Zack killed him. It was his prescription that Adrian OD'ed on." She says, her eyes flashing with a cruelty I don't understand.

"You're lying." The words escape from between clenched teeth, low and murderous.

Lauren laughs, the sound shrill, piercing the air like a hyena. "You're cute. What? You thought he was interested in you? Or cared about you? Maura, the only reason Zack's hanging out with you is because he feels guilty. Adrian's overdose is his fault and now, he feels sorry for you."

My stomach sinks at her words, a coldness sweeping through my veins.

Is she telling the truth?

Does Zack feel sorry for me?

Was everything between us a lie?

"If you're telling the truth, why didn't you tell me earlier? Why tell me now?"

"Because now, you're causing issues for Zack and me. Before, I didn't care about you one way or the other. Now, I need you to understand that you'll never be anything more than a charity case to Zack. Back off so we can be together again. Without you as a distraction."

Charity case.

Her word choice hit its mark, causing my doubts to burst from a flicker to a flame.

Still, some of old Maura must lurk inside because instead of showing her how much her words hurt me, I roll my eyes and snort. "You're just jealous. Go home Lauren; your desperation is showing."

Picking up my bag, I stride past her, my head held high.

But once I'm in the safety of my dorm, the insecurities surge forth, like the breaking of a dam.

Am I a charity case? Is that how Zack sees me?

Who really gave Adrian the pills that caused his overdose?

Sinking onto my bed, I pick at the new comforter set I bought from Walmart.

She's lying. Lauren doesn't know what she's talking about.

Zack wouldn't do that, would he?

I need a drink.

Rummaging through my bag, I pull out the bottle of wine that Lila's mom gave me for Thanksgiving.

Thank God it's a screw top and not a cork. Twisting the cap, I fill a red Solo cup and swallow the contents.

The bold red bursts in my veins, calming my nerves and warming my blood with each mouthful. Flipping on the TV, I tune into re-runs of *Keeping Up with the Kardashians*. Between the wine and the reality TV, my mind begins to quiet.

Two episodes later, I'm halfway through the wine bottle.

Kourtney Kardashian gives birth to Penelope.

And the tears come.

At first they start as a small trickle of wetness gliding down my cheeks. I brush them away impatiently with the backs of my hands. However, they refuse to quit and within moments, I'm sobbing, straight up ugly crying, with snot dripping from my nostrils and my mouth hanging open with tragic sounds escaping.

Picking up the phone, I dial Emma.

Voicemail.

I try again. And again. After the fourth attempt, I bury my face in my pillow and let the tears fall until I feel completely, overwhelmingly empty.

"You're too sexy for this place, baby." A guy catcalls to me as I wander into a club.

Flipping him off, I snake through throngs of people, swaying couples, and giggling girls without touching a single soul. Loud music, a dark and seedy atmosphere, the pulsing swarm of bodies on the verge of bad decisions; I'm back, bitch.

"Rum and Coke." I shout to a bartender.

The first taste hits the back of my throat, loosening some of the ice in my chest. Swirling the little black straw around and around in my glass, I lean my shoulder blades against the top of the bar and watch the dance floor. Like I did last month.

I'm pathetic.

Who comes to a club alone?

I take another gulp of my drink.

The song changes and a salsa beat picks up. My hips automatically sway to the music, my hair moving over my shoulders. A guy places his hands on my hips, drawing me into the crowd. I toss back the rest of my beverage and hand him the empty glass with the ice cubes rattling around. I'm not sure what he does with it but once it's discarded, I'm wrapped in his arms, waiting for the numbness to return.

Twirling around the dance floor, I pass from one guy to the next. Sweat gleams off my skin as I grind against whoever is holding me from behind.

"Why aren't you answering my calls?" he murmurs in my ear.

Spinning, I look up into Hector's face. "What are you doing here?"

"Same thing as you." He steps closer, his hands gripping

my hips, his familiar scent clogging my throat. "Why are you letting every man in here have a piece of you when you could have hit me up?"

"Felt like it."

"You're angry tonight." He grins, pulling me into his sweaty frame and pressing against me. "I like feisty Maura."

"Screw you, Hector."

"What do you think I'm trying to do here?"

"I learned the truth about Adrian's death." I push against his meaty shoulders.

Hector winces, stepping back. "Jesus, Maura. I'm sorry, okay? That why you're dodging me?"

"You're sorry?"

Hector swears. From his expression, he thinks I'm being a smartass. Wrapping my hand around two of his fingers, I tug him off the dance floor and out a side entrance of the club.

"Damn, Maura, it's like two degrees outside." He complains, his expression hard.

"You're sorry?" I repeat, waiting for him to fill in the blanks that are firing around my mind.

"Adrian was using, okay? I hooked him up with some Percocet and Vicodin. Whenever he was in a pinch, I'd help him out. The last time, shit was laced, a bad batch." He shrugs, as if he lost out on a two-dollar scratch off lottery ticket and not my brother's life.

"You sold my brother drugs?" Disbelief laces my tone and Hector shuffles back a step.

"You didn't know?"

"You killed Adrian!" I shriek, my hand striking him across the face.

He grabs my wrist, squeezing until I swear I hear my bones creak. Getting up into my face, he pushes his forehead against mine. "That was your one hit, you understand? Don't go fucking loco on me because your brother was a druggie. He knew the risks; he took them anyway."

"Is that why you were banging me?"

He snorts, low and breathless. "I fucked you because you're good in bed. And yeah, we have history, childhood good times; it was good seeing you not look like someone shot your dog."

"My twin is dead."

I'm going to be sick.

What the hell is happening?

Did I not know Adrian at all?

I can't breathe.

The last thought causes me to suck in a mouthful of oxygen, but it doesn't enter my lungs quickly enough and floaters appear in my vision.

"Shit." Hector mutters. "Grow up, Maura. Your brother's shit was his own business. You and I had a good run, but I can't deal with this shit. Take care of yourself. And get a goddamn jacket." He pushes past me, disappearing back inside the club.

Standing in the freezing cold, I look around the dark night. Nothing makes any sense.

Nothing.

Stone cold sober from Hector's words, a lucidity that cuts in its sharpness fills my mind. My body trembles, my breaths puncturing the night air like cigarette smoke.

Surrounded by the foreboding night sky and the paralyzing cold, I should be scared. But I'm too numb to feel anything, even emotion.

Wandering around the streets of Philadelphia, I search for some sign of truth before I dial his number.

"Hello?"

"We need to talk."

"Maura?" I hold the phone several inches away to double check her name on the screen. 3AM. *What the hell?* "You okay?"

"That depends."

"Maura, where are you?"

"On a sidewalk."

"Where did you go tonight?" Jealousy glares through my tone and I don't care. *Who is she with at 3AM?*

"Out. Needed to drink, dance, get lost for a while."

"Where are you?"

"I'm asking the questions, Zack."

I slip from my bed and tug on a pair of sweats. "Come over."

After several seconds of silence, she sighs and I hear the emotion behind her breath. "Answer your door."

Panic flickers at the edges of my mind.

Does she know?

Heading downstairs, I pace in the foyer, thoughts buzzing through my mind.

Is Maura drunk?

She wasn't slurring.

Did something happen with one of her friends?

Is she hurt?

Jesus, it could be anything!

Terror and relief seize my chest when she knocks on the front door and I pull it wide open.

"Maura." I reach for her, unnerved when she shakes off my touch and steps inside my house.

She smells like sweet rum and her usual spicy heat. Her hair is wild and her cheeks are flushed, whether from sitting in the cold or drinking too many Captain Morgan's or —

"I need a water."

"Sure." I lead her into the kitchen, flipping on the lights, and filling her a water glass.

We sit at my kitchen table, the silence heavy between us.

"Everything okay?"

She shrugs, her fingers drawing shapes in the condensation on the water glass.

"Where'd you go tonight?" I bite the inside of my cheek as I drink in her short skirt and backless shirt. I hate the thought that she spent the night with a guy. *Did he put his hands on her, kiss her? And where is he now?*

"Club Azure. Felt like dancing."

"Did you have fun?"

"I need to ask you a question."

"What is it?"

"And I need you to be completely honest with me."

My heart stops. My limbs lock down. Dread rolls through my veins. "What?"

"Did you give my brother drugs?"

40

MAURA

Z ack's looking at me like I throat punched him.

Disheveled blond hair, piercing blue eyes, a sexy build, and none of it can detract from the horror that blooms in his expression.

Bile rises in my throat and a coldness I've never experienced sweeps through my body, chilling me. *He gave Adrian pills. He knew Adrian was using. He —*

"I'm sorry. Maura, I —"

"Yes or no, Zack?" My words crack and Zack flinches.

"Yes." He whispers, his eyes pleading.

I begin to push back from the table but his hand clamps down on my wrist, halting my departure.

"I didn't know. Not at first." His eyes bleed with anguish, his voice low. "I had a Vicodin prescription from a knee surgery. It had a few refills on it and suddenly, I was short two. I couldn't remember filling the prescription but figured I was overthinking it. But then Adrian started complaining about back pain and acting differently."

I sit down in my chair. My body is coiled so tightly, my muscles ache from the strain.

"I can't explain exactly what was off; he just wasn't himself. I kept asking him about his back, and then one day, he said he was good. He said he got help for it. I thought he was seeing a physical therapist, getting massages, whatever. But then I found a prescription bottle on his desk for Vicodin. In my name. And I blew up at him, confronted him about the whole thing. I was furious with him, yelling how he was fucking up his future. I cancelled the remaining prescriptions and he left the house with us cursing each other out. And he never came home."

"Zack."

"You were right; I killed him. It's my fault he's dead."

Shaking my head, I try to make sense of the information overload I received today. *Lauren. Hector. Zack.*

Three versions of the same story.

But only Zack looks devastated, like he lost a piece of himself the day he lost Adrian.

"Lauren told me you gave him pills."

"Lauren?"

"I didn't know if she was telling the truth or just being Lauren."

"She was telling the truth."

"No, she wasn't." I shift closer to him, placing a tentative hand on his forearm.

"Maura, it was my prescription that —"

"He got the pills he OD'ed on from Hector."

"Who the hell is Hector?"

"A guy from our old neighborhood that I —"

"Teardrop tattoos?"

I nod, my throat closing with shame. "I've been screwing the guy who sold Adrian laced drugs; how messed up is that?"

Zack winces at my words, hurt slashing across his face. "I'm sorry, Maura."

"I don't blame you, Zack. God, I wished so hard for someone to blame but really, there's no one except Adrian. And that hurts."

"I should have prevented it; I should have done something."

"Stop! Adrian stole from you, lied to you, and got more pills from another source when he knew you wouldn't let him get away with it. That's not on you."

"But I did let him get away with it." Anger wraps around Zack's words, exasperation in the lines of his face. "I'm responsible for his death! If he didn't find my bottle of Vicodin, if I'd been more careful about the refills, if I'd followed up with the pharmacist, he'd still be here! He wouldn't have gone to Hector. I could have helped him get real help. I was just too scared, too goddamn cowardly to confront my best friend and accuse him of stealing from me. And then when I did, he fucking died!" Zack's yelling now, his hands puncturing the air.

"No." I shake my head, grabbing his wrist. "That's bullshit, Zack. You were his best friend. And he deceived you. If they weren't your pills, they would have been someone else's. Hell, he could have been stealing pills from one of my uncle's medicine cabinets, from other guys on the team, buying them off class-mates, and just keeping them in the bottle with your name on it." My body begins to shake with anger, then sadness, as tears erupt from my chest like a volcano. "I wanted it to be you! I wanted to be so goddamn angry with you. But then I saw Hector and he admitted everything without even flinching. And you, you're carrying around all this guilt, drowning in it, when it wasn't even your fault. It wasn't anyone's fault except Adrian's." I blow out, swiping a hand over my face to collect the tears. "I'm so angry all the time. And I hate it. I hate being angry at a dead person. Why would he do something so stupid? Why wouldn't he tell me?"

Zack reaches forward and pulls me into his chest, his arms holding me as I cry, his hands twisting in my curls.

"Baby, please, don't cry. I'm sorry. I hate seeing you in so much pain. I hate seeing you with random guys, drinking and partying, trying to feel again. I hate that I did this to you."

Charity case.

Lauren's words from earlier seep into my consciousness, twisting my stomach until I gag. Jerking away from Zack's touch, I gasp. "Oh my God."

"What?"

"That's it, isn't it?"

"What are you talking about? What's it?"

"That's why you're hanging out with me. Because you feel guilty. Because you feel sorry for me. I'm just Adrian's pitiful sister who can't get past his death and you're trying to lessen the guilt you feel. It's not about me at all. It's about you." I push off of his forearms, standing from my chair so quickly, it tips over.

"Are you kidding me? It's always been about you, about what I feel for you. Maura, wait!"

Embarrassment burns my skin as I rush to the front door.

How could I have been so stupid?

Lauren was right; Zack could never be interested in me.

He's seen too much of my ugly.

Lauren. Hector. Zack.

Too much for twenty-four hours.

My body is crashing, my mind on overdrive.

I reach for the doorknob as Zack's hand shoots out, holding the door closed.

"Baby, please." He spins me around in his arms, pulling me up onto my toes, his eyes searing into mine.

Pain and anguish connect us, a thread pulled so tightly, it snaps. A growl escapes Zack's throat just as his lips crash over mine.

He kisses me. Hard, with purpose, with abandon.

And it swallows me whole. The way I always knew it would.

My body betrays me as my fingers claw up his arms to reach his shoulders. I arch into him, and he drags me closer, his hands lost in my hair as I drown in him. His tongue dances with mine wildly, passionately. And just when I think I can't take anymore, he gentles the kiss, slows the pace. My heels return to the ground, the tension in his arms relax, and I melt into him like watercolor paints: slowly, sweetly, beautifully.

"It's always been about you." He breaks our kiss, dropping his forehead to mine, and framing my face between his palms. "If anything, I was petrified that telling you the truth would make you hate me, would make me lose you. And that was selfish. Because, Maura, I feel so fucking much for you that I couldn't handle it if you ever hated me."

"I could never hate you, Zack."

"I'm so sorry for everything."

A hurricane of sadness and grief sweeps through my body. All of the tears I've cried, the bargains I've made with God, somersault through my stomach, up my throat, until I open my mouth and let them go. I offer Zack the words he needs to hear; I tell him the truth. "I forgive you. Now you need to forgive yourself."

His eyes shutter closed, a sigh falling from his lips. Pressing a kiss to my forehead, he murmurs. "So do you, baby. So do you."

"Can I stay with you tonight?" The words tumble from my mouth. As desperate as I was to escape Zack's house just moments ago, that kiss, that confession, changed things. And I'm too keyed up, too emotionally overwhelmed, too emotionally drained, too confused to be on my own tonight.

I don't want to get lost with him tonight to feel numb.

I want to discover myself through him to feel everything.

My skin literally aches for his touch. I want to sleep tangled up with him, wake up slowly in the morning, splayed against his chest, counting the beats of his heart. "Please."

He brushes a kiss across my lips and, without hesitation, says the single greatest word in the English language. At least in this moment. "Always."

41

ZACK

C losing my bedroom door behind Maura, I'm shocked that she's here. In my room. With me.

Tonight has been crazy and its finally nearing sunrise.

Pulling out a T-shirt, I hand it to her so she can get comfortable.

She grins at me, pulling her shirt up, over her head, and discarding it on the floor. Tugging her skirt down, it pools at her feet, and she steps out of it.

Jesus.

Clad in a lacy black bra and thong, Maura sashays toward me and my mouth dries.

She's the most beautiful woman I've ever seen.

My fingers itch to touch her, my body already reacting to the sight of her smooth skin, the pout of her full mouth. But my head hurls logic at me too loudly to ignore.

"Wait." I reach out, halting her approach. "Not tonight."

"Are you seriously turning me down right now?"

"You have absolutely no idea how badly I want you right now. My body and mind are screaming at me to shut the fuck up."

"Then what's the problem?"

I groan, sinking to the edge of my bed and tugging her down beside me. My palm splays in the center of her back, her skin like silk. "I care about you, Maura. I've cared about you for a long time. And I want to start things between us the right way."

She grins, her eyes dazzling. "What does that even mean? The right way?"

"I'm glad you're amused by my trying to be serious."

"The right way? You sound about ninety."

"I want to undress you slowly, kiss you senseless, and keep you in my bed for days. But not after you've been out drinking, needing to make sense of things. Not after we hashed things out about Adrian. Not after you brought up Hector. When we get together, it better be just about us. You and me. With no one else in the room."

Her eyes darken, blacker than midnight, deeper than endless. "Okay."

Pressing my T-shirt into her hand, I grin, "For tonight, all we do is sleep."

Maura pulls the T-shirt over her head and scoots to the top of my bed. Pulling down the duvet cover, I flip it over her and slide into bed beside her, turning off the light.

Placing my face next to hers on the pillow, my hand finds hers underneath the sheets, linking our fingers together. "Sweet dreams, Maura."

"Goodnight, Zack."

WHEN I OPEN my eyes the next morning, I'm greeted by Maura's sleeping face pressed against the pillow, a snore whistling through her nose each time she exhales. Her hair is twisted into a bun on top of her head, messy curls springing free as she snuggles deeper under the covers. A pillow line creases her cheek and her lips purse as though deep in thought. She's completely adorable, and I remain still, hesitant to wake her.

After several minutes of observing her sleeping form, I really need to take a piss and my body is aching to stretch. Carefully, I push back my side of the covers and slip out of bed. She doesn't move.

Chuckling to myself at how sweet and peaceful she looks asleep, I miss the sarcastic quip on the edge of her tongue. After using the bathroom and pulling on some sweats, I walk around the corner to find us some coffee and bagels for breakfast.

Ice patches gleam in the sunlight and the air is frigid, whipping against my cheeks as I hunch forward and stuff my hands deep into my pockets. Walking half a block, I pop into the nearest bagel shop and inhale, the scent of fresh baked bagels and brewing coffee surrounding me.

"Hey, man, what can I get for you?"

"Hey. Two coffees please, milk in both, no sugar. And two egg, cheese, and pork roll on everything bagels."

"Salt, pepper, ketchup?"

"Yup."

"Twelve seventy."

I hand him a twenty and wait for my change.

He hands me the coffees. "The sandwiches will be five minutes."

"Great, thanks." I walk over to one of the corner tables, taking a seat by the window. It's 8:30 AM meaning it's 7:30 AM at home, meaning Nicole could use a wake-up call. I pull out my phone and give her a ring, taking a sip of the scalding coffee and wincing as I burn my tongue.

"Hello?" Her voice is groggy and thick with sleep.

"Wake your ass up!"

"What the hell is wrong with you and what do you want?"

"Nothing is wrong with me. I'm awesome. Just wanted to see how you're doing."

"This is payback, isn't it? For all the times I've called you when you were already asleep, your alarm set for 5:00 AM."

"Maybe. So, what're you up to this weekend?"

Nicole groans again but I sense she's waking up since she starts right in on me. "Did you do it yet?"

"Do what?"

"Ask Maura out."

"Kind of. You were right. You can hang it over my head for all of eternity."

"Obviously, we always knew I was right. That wasn't even up for debate. What the hell does 'kind of' mean?"

"I sense the gossip gleam shining in your eyes like a crazy, deranged person."

"Shut up and spill it."

I take another sip of the scalding coffee. "Maura and I talked. But we didn't actually conclude anything."

"How'd it go down?"

"She showed up at my house last night."

"And?"

"And we talked, really talked. And discussed a lot of things about Adrian that needed to be said."

"But you're happy?" My sister's voice turns serious, and I grin. Nicole, for all her antics and irritating ways, always has my back, and always wants the best for me.

"Yeah, Nic, I'm happy. What else is going on by you?"

We chat for a few more minutes as Nicole fills me in on Mom and Dad and tells me about a date she has with some hotshot lawyer this weekend. The guy from Halloween never panned out. When I hang up the phone, I'm cheesing way too hard, which has everything to do with the text message on my screen. And the girl who sent it.

Maura: Morning sunshine! Where'd you disappear to?

MAURA and I spend the remainder of the day under the covers in my bed, carb-loading and binge-watching *House of Cards* on Netflix. Every now and then we discuss the episodes, compare stories on what we predict will happen next, or make general observations.

"Maura?" I interrupt whatever Francis Underwood is saying on screen.

"Yeah?" She looks over at me, and I guess I look serious because she pauses the episode. "What's up?"

"I just ... I want to make sure we're on the same page. After last night?"

She grins, a wicked gleam in her eyes. "And what page is that?"

"You really are a pain in the ass. You're going to make me say it." I swear, she is unlike any girl I've ever met. Every girl I know would be clamoring for some type of reassurance this morning but Maura Rodriguez has me playing the typical chick role.

"I have a great ass and of course I'm going to make you say it."

"I love your ass." I grab a handful and squeeze until she snickers. "But seriously, I know you're not ready to be in a relationship."

She looks down for a beat before meeting my gaze and nodding.

"And that's fine. I don't know what we are but it doesn't

matter because I know how I feel about you. So I just need you to know that I'm here for you and I'm waiting and whenever you're ready, I want to give us a real shot."

"Me too." She snuggles deeper into my side. "I'm sorry I'm so fucked-up."

"You're not fucked-up, baby. You're grieving."

"Still. I don't want you to think I don't want to be with you. Because I do."

"Let's just take it slow."

She glances up at me beneath her dark lashes. "So we just take it one day at a time?" The incredulity in her voice causes me to pause. *Has any guy ever been decent to her?*

"One day at a time," I echo.

She kisses the top of my shoulder. "Okay."

I nod and press play to resume the episode.

After that, we sink into a comfortable silence, where words don't need to be spoken because we know where we stand with each other. Before I leave that night, Maura asks me to have dinner with her the following day. "Sure," I tell her casually, but really I'm relieved. We're definitely heading in the right direction.

DECEMBER

42

MAURA

I wake on the first of December to a light dusting of snow as snowflakes flurry from the sky.

It's cold outside, the kind of cold that hurts your chest when you breathe in too deep, and I savor the feeling as I clutch a hot cup of Starbucks Peppermint Mocha between my hands. An energy, an excitement, a new sense of hopefulness flows through me as my boots crunch through the snow on my way to practice. We've been practicing indoors for a few weeks now and it's a quick walk to the gym where the Erg room is located. This allows me an extra fifteen minutes of sleep in the morning, which makes a big difference in my life.

"Hi, Kay." I sip the last of my drink and discard the paper cup in a nearby recycling bin. "What're we doing today?" I ask, replacing my boots for sneakers.

"Hey, Maura. One under intervals followed by thirty minutes steady. It's not too bad," she replies before sitting next to me and lacing up her sneakers.

I nod, thinking over our workout and calculating what my heart rate should be throughout the intervals.

"Our times are improving. I think Holy Cross and Wakefield are going to be our biggest competitors going into the spring season."

"Yeah our times are definitely better, but I think we need to switch up our start to compete with Wakefield. They're start is really powerful and they managed to take the lead from the get-go in a lot of the fall regattas."

"What do you have in mind?" She asks, her eyes curious.

We talk crew, stats, starts. Just like we used to.

Before.

The rest of the team files in throughout our conversation. The girls remove heavy layers of jackets, sweatshirts, hats, and boots. By the time we've assembled onto our ergs and Kay has written the workout on the whiteboard at the front of the room, it feels like I'm back.

Maura the rower, the athlete, the winner.

Just in time for winter training.

Practice passes quickly, and I finish the sets with strong times. I'm pleased with my performance and a bit relieved that after so many months of slacking off, I'm still able to compete at a decent level. I'm nowhere near where I was, or where I should be, but I'll get there. I'm committed now so things are different.

After practice, I toe off my sneakers and slide back into my boots. Picking up my practice bag, I check my phone and grin that there's a message from Zack.

Zack: Good morning, bet your up before the sun. Snow's already sticking. Want to do dinner in the form of takeout tonight instead?

Me: Sure, sounds good. Come to my dorm around 7?

He responds instantly.

Zack: I'll be there. Italian OK?

Me: Perfect. Xo

"Oh wow, Maura, what's with the smile?" Valerie calls

me out, nudging Amanda in her side. "Get a look at Rodriguez's face. Who's the guy?"

I blush.

Several other teammates look at me now, and the girls laugh.

"I have a date tonight," I confess.

Kay whistles loudly and hysterics erupt again.

"Good for you," Valerie says seriously. "It's about time a boy made you smile like that."

Casey nods in agreement. "Yeah. It's about time you smile in general."

Amber snorts.

"Quit it!" I say but I'm cheesing too hard. Shouldering my duffle bag, I flip them off.

"Hope to not see you suckers tomorrow morning."

Everyone laughs except Kay. "We'll still have practice. The snow won't be that bad."

"Yeah, okay, Hillard." Valerie rolls her eyes. "Have fun tonight, Maura."

I wave a hand in farewell and head out of the gym to my Photography class.

BY THE TIME DUSK FALLS, the snow is several inches high and patches of black ice hide along the pathways around McShain. Weather forecasters are predicting eight to ten inches of snow tonight. Hopefully classes, and maybe even practice, will be cancelled in the morning. I'm relieved Zack had the foresight to reschedule our dinner plans so we didn't have to cancel. It's embarrassing how excited I am to see him tonight. Things are different now; I'm getting to the place I need to be in for us to be together. Like a real couple. And he's patiently waiting. Like the good guy I don't deserve but am relieved to have a chance with.

I'm really freaking happy and the thought is somewhat unsettling as I realize how unhappy I've been for so long. Living in a fog, going through the motions, getting through the day.

Not anymore. Now, it's like I'm waking up after a really long sleep, viewing my surroundings in a new light, embracing a new perspective.

Being happy is actually a relief.

My FaceTime rings as Mia's name flashes on the screen.

"Ciao Mia!"

"Hi! How are you?"

"Good, you? You look happy," I comment, noting her bright eyes and wide smile.

"So do you." She shoots back before tilting her head to study me. "You look different too. What's going on?"

I shrug.

"Spill it, Maura."

"I have a date."

Mia's mouth drops open. "With who?"

"Zack."

Confusion crosses her face. "Do I know him?"

"Kind of."

Mia narrows her eyes, pursing her lips in thought. "Adrian's friend?"

"Ding, ding, ding."

"Oh my God." A hand covers her mouth in surprise. "When did this happen? I thought he was just like, looking out for you or something."

"Yeah, me too. But it sort of … I don't know, developed into more. Is that bad?" I ask, desperate for Mia's reassurance that I'm not doing something wrong by falling for Adrian's best friend.

"No! Not at all. I think it's really amazing. It's great that you've found someone that understands everything you've been going through and also has a connection to Adrian. It's perfect really. You guys already have so much in common plus a shared history, you know?"

"Yeah. I think Adrian would approve."

"Are you kidding me? Adrian would totally approve. Once he got past the shock that his best friend was into his sister. What are you guys doing tonight?"

"Hanging in and eating takeout. We're getting a blizzard." I roll my eyes.

"Sweet!" Mia's face lights up, "I hope you guys get snowed in and rowing is cancelled."

"From your mouth to God's ears."

"I'll light a candle for you at the Vatican."

"You're a true friend. What's new with you and the Italiano?"

"So much to tell you! But I actually have to go. I was just calling to say hi. I promise, once I'm back in a few weeks, we're going to have a real, serious catch-up. And I'll share everything then."

I roll my eyes but nod, resigning myself to the fact that I'll have to be out of the loop a little longer. I guess the details don't matter as long as my best friend is as happy as she is. "Okay, but I'm holding you to that."

"Promise." She places a hand over her heart. "See you soon?"

"Yes! I can't even wait."

"Me too. Bye, Maura!" She blows a kiss.

"Later, Mia." I press the red button to disconnect our call.

Shuffling over to my desk, I pick up the framed photo of

the four of us and study our faces. Lila's eyes are open and shining, her blond waves tumbling around her shoulders. Emma's mouth is half-open in a laugh, her hand coming up to insist on another photo. Mia looks nervous, her chocolate eyes serious, her smile hesitant. And me, I look ... like a shadow of myself. My mouth is twisted between a smile and a snarl and my eyes are turbulent with all the things I didn't know how to express, all the anger I held onto before I started confiding in Zack.

It's amazing really, how much four months can change your life. How much being on your own for the first time ever does force you to grow, look at aspects of yourself and be honest about the person you are. I thought this semester would be lonely and boring, that I would meddle through a routine I've done for years. I thought I wouldn't learn anything, wouldn't stick to the pact, wouldn't even venture out of my comfort zone. Because while the other girls were seeking out adventure and a new journey, I was going back. Back to the familiar, to the known, to the consistency.

What the hell could be challenging about that?

I thought I'd sink into the numbness I craved until the spring semester rolled around so I could thaw out like frost.

But then Zack happened.

He forced me to confront things I was avoiding, like my anger toward Adrian. He made me realize that being numb is sometimes harder than being hurt. The repercussions last longer.

He made me feel optimistic again, hopeful for the future. And I forgot how amazing it feels just to revel in being alive, eager to begin another day, positive about the unknown.

Zack redefined my comfort zone.

43

ZACK

I knock on Maura's door a little after 7:00 PM, a brown bag of Italian takeout in my hand, a small Margherita pizza balancing between the wall and my forearm.

She opens the door, her smile shy. She's dressed in tight black yoga pants and a large, oversized sweater that slides off her left shoulder, revealing her smooth caramel skin. "Hi."

"You look beautiful."

She rolls her eyes and reaches forward to take the pizza off my arm. "Come on in."

My eyes drink her in. The curve of her tight ass in those pants, the slope of her neck as her sweater slides down farther, the tangle of black curls that sit in a bun on top of her head.

She's stunning and the crazy thing is, she has absolutely no clue.

Sure, she knows she's sexy when she's trying to be angry, sarcastic, hard Maura. But under that fragile surface, she's sweet and kind and hurting. And so fucking real that her rawness, her unapologetic honesty, her truth is so damn beautiful, it's blinding. And when I stare at her, I have to remind myself to blink, to breathe, to respond to whatever she's saying in this moment.

"What?" I ask, coming back to the moment.

"I asked what did you bring for dinner? Besides pizza."

"Oh." I hold up the bag still dangling from my hand. "Pasta primavera and seafood risotto."

"Mmm." She groans appreciatively, her tongue darting out to slide along her bottom lip. "I'm starving."

"Me too." I cross the threshold and close the door behind me.

The second the latch catches, the room shifts. The gravity of this moment sinks in. After all the uncertainty and bad timing of this semester, things are finally falling together instead of apart.

"Go to Boston with me," I blurt out, watching her eyes widen in surprise.

"What?"

I step forward, placing the takeout bag on her desk and taking her hand in mine. "I know this sounds crazy. But I want to eat crab cakes with you and do something fun and spontaneous. Winter break is in a few weeks. Before we head home for Christmas, let's go to Boston. We'll freeze our asses off and eat New England clam chowder in bread bowls. We'll be tourists and walk the Freedom Trail, visit Paul Revere's house, and lurk in cemeteries at dusk. We'll get away from all of this," I throw my arm out, gesturing to McShain University, and Boathouse Row, and the entire city of Philadelphia, "and just be me and you and see where that leads us."

Silence.

Oh, shit.

Did I push too hard?

Too soon?

It's too damn late now.

And then Maura smiles and it's like the sun peeking through the clouds, brightening her entire face. "Okay."

"Seriously?"

"Seriously. I'm embracing the college pact."

"The what?"

"A thing. I'm meant to be brave."

"You're the bravest woman I know."

"Thanks, but I never left. And I want to, need to do something outside my predictable routine."

"So we'll go to Boston?"

"We'll go to Boston."

Grinning, I place my hands on Maura's hips and pull her flush against my chest. Wrapping my arms around her, I kiss her until her stomach grumbles.

"You said Italian, right?" she steps back, her eyes dancing.

"Good to know you'd rather eat than kiss me." I swat her ass.

"Priorities." She lays out a blanket in the middle of her bedroom floor and sets up a picnic. "Thanks for bringing takeout."

"Thanks for the impromptu picnic." I hold up my plastic fork to her. "Cheers."

"To Boston."

"To us."

"Snow day!" Maura announces the following morning, dancing around like a kid in her thermal pajamas. "And no practice!"

I laugh, settling back against the pillows. "Then come back to bed." I hold my arm out toward her.

"Don't you have to check to see if you have practice?"

"Nah, Phillips anticipated this happening. We all have to get a workout in today at the gym but it's whatever we feel like doing and at whatever time we feel like doing it."

"Lucky! I wish Kay gave us that option. What about your classes?"

"Come back to bed."

She complies and I tuck her under my arm. We almost never have the luxury of sleeping in, and I don't want to waste one more minute of it talking when I could be falling asleep with Maura in my arms. Luckily, sleep drags us both under in minutes.

When I wake for the second time, Maura is already awake, sitting at her desk, typing furiously on her laptop, her bottom lip tucked between her teeth.

"Are you seriously doing homework?" I ask, pressing up on my forearm and combing my fingers through my tangled hair.

"I thought I'd make the most out of the time you spent snoozing so we could hang when you wake up."

"Smart thinking. I guess I'll just blow off all my assignments?"

She turns in her chair to face me. "You're the one who insisted on sleeping in." She points a pen at my chest. "Now that you're awake, want to dig our way through the snow to the dining hall? I'm starving."

I run a hand down my face. I really need to shave and shower and look like a person again but the chance to spend extra time with Maura trumps everything. "Sure." Swinging my legs over the side of her bed, I rake my hair into a messy bun at the back of my head.

"I really like your hair."

I raise an eyebrow at her.

"It suits you, although a man-bun is not something I would picture you with based off your personality."

I chuckle. "What do you mean by that?"

"I don't know. Man-buns are like trendy and edgy. And you're sweet and stable."

"Well, I hate to burst your bubble but you're probably right. I've been wearing my hair long, at least to my collarbone, for years. Before it became a fad. So … there's that."

She snorts. "I like it though. It's sexy."

"I'm glad you think so, Rodriguez. Let's go." I stand up, pulling on my sweatpants. "I'm letting you buy my breakfast with your meal plan." I pick up her student ID from her nightstand.

We shuffle through the cold to the dining hall, careful not to step on any icy patches. Once we're inside, we fill our plates high with scrambled eggs, bacon, and hash browns. I grab us coffees and we settle our trays on a table next to the window. Beneath us a large expanse of soft, white snow blankets the campus.

"It's pretty, isn't it?" Maura asks, her eyes trained outside.

"Yeah. It's nice actually, being a normal student for once and sleeping in, having a snow day, coming to the dining hall at," I check my Fitbit, "11:30 AM for breakfast."

"I know what you mean. I feel like a kid whenever we have snow days."

"So, tell me about this crazy adventure you're meant to be having this semester." I shovel scrambled eggs into my mouth. "What's the deal with that?"

"Stupid college pact," she rolls her eyes, filling me in on the agreement she made with Mia, Emma, and Lila at the beginning of the semester.

"I get that. That's cool, actually, that you guys are all trying to make the most of your semester apart." I toss a hash brown in her direction. "You're not, like, mailing a pair of jeans between the four of you or anything, right?"

She snorts. "Hardly. But, the more important question is, how the hell do you even know about *The Sisterhood of the Traveling Pants*?"

"Busted." I groan. "Nicole. She loved that book and then made us all watch the movie. Did you know there's a sequel?"

"Oh my God! You're so lame!"

"But in a good way, right?"

"In the best way." She grins, eating the bacon off my plate.

THE NEXT SEVERAL days pass quickly as Maura and I settle into a routine. We both rise early for rowing, head to our respective practices, attend our classes, lock ourselves in the library to prepare for finals, and spend each night wrapped up in the warmth of each other as we fall into deep, peaceful sleeps.

In the moments before we both pass out, our eyes heavy with exhaustion, we tell each other about our days, share funny stories, confide about things that are bothering us. And sometimes, we sit in comfortable silence until one of us dozes off and the other quickly follows.

Ending each night, I drink in her profile, watch her chest rise and fall with each breath, and note the pout of her full lips.

Even though I'm counting down to our weekend in Boston, I'm also cherishing these quiet moments where the two of us exist side by side in the certainty that our futures are intertwined.

44

MAURA

I really, really want to have sex.

Edit: I need to have sex.

Zack has slept over every night since December started. He wraps me in his arms, tangles his warm legs with mine, and kisses my lips, my cheeks, my neck.

And then he wishes me goodnight.

And I need to catapult us to the next stage in our relationship.

Like, yesterday.

Even though we haven't said the words yet, I want to be his girlfriend.

I want him to be my boyfriend.

I want us to be in an exclusive, monogamous relationship.

And, sex!

Just the stroke of his hand over my hair or the press of his lips to the back of my neck before I drop into sleep has my senses waking, my nerves zinging, my body craving his touch in a way I've never experienced before. And it's not because I want to be numb, but rather I want him to light me up like a firework and let me burn out like a shooting star.

I want *him*.

But how the hell do I say that without sounding like some horny freak? I mean, I blush just thinking about the guys Zack has seen me with, the bad decisions he's witnessed me make. And I don't want him to think I'm just in it for the sex. Because I'm not. But hell if I'm not craving it, craving him, something fierce.

So, I turn to the master of these predicaments and she answers on the first ring.

"Hey girl, hey." Emma waves on FaceTime.

"Emma! How are you?"

She narrows her eyes. "Why are you so chipper?"

"No reason."

"Mia tells me you had a date."

"I'm kind of with someone."

Her eyebrows shoot up, disappearing under her bangs. "How are you kind of with someone and not really with someone? And more importantly, who is he? And most importantly, how come I'm just hearing about this now?"

"All good questions."

"You can start answering in any order you feel most comfortable with." She smirks, settling back against the cushions of her couch.

"Gee, thanks. Let's see, it's Zack, Adrian's best friend."

Emma coughs on the water bottle she just took a drink from. "Huntington?"

"Yeah. You have a good memory."

"Holy shit. You're getting it on with Zack Huntington? That boy is deliciously sexy. Not to mention a good guy. Wow, Maura, way to go!"

"And herein lies the issue."

"Huh?" Emma looks at me like I'm crazy. "What issue?"

"We're not 'getting it on.' We're snuggling!"

Emma's mouth falls open as she cracks up. She smacks her hand over her mouth, but the laughter continues, her eyes squeezing shut as she falls sideways on the couch. "Oh my God. Stop! Are you kidding me?"

"Stop laughing." I scold her. "I'm calling you for advice, not to be your entertainment."

"Hold up. Go back to the beginning. How are you kind of but not really together?"

"We started hanging out as friends and then it sort of just developed from there. But we're not like boyfriend-girlfriend or anything."

"But you want to be?"

"Yes. We're going to Boston together after my last final."

"What?" Her eyes widen. "This is so for real!"

"God, I hope so."

"Wait, why didn't you tell me about this sooner?"

"I didn't know if it was for real. I thought I was pining for him and he was being nice to me out of respect for Adrian, and I don't know, it didn't seem like something worth mentioning until it actually became something."

"Fair. I'm letting you off the hook because that actually makes sense."

"Advice, please."

"Do you think he wants to make it official before y'all, you know, do it?"

I tilt my head to the left, considering her words. "I don't know. He's kind of old-fashioned sometimes; I mean, he's from Nebraska." I grin, thinking about how annoyed he would be at my assumption.

"That means nothing." Emma chides me.

"I know. I just like teasing him. But I do think he wants us to be in a real relationship before escalating things."

"Or maybe he just really cares about you and is waiting for you to make the first move?"

"Maybe." I tilt my head to the right. Yeah, I could see Zack waiting for a cue from me to make sure I'm comfortable with increasing the physicality of our relationship.

"You know what I think you should do?"

"What?"

"Talk to him and be honest."

"Ugh." I groan, face-palming myself. "Why didn't I think of that?" I shake my head, cutting her a look. "Obviously I don't want to come right out and say it, and that's why I'm asking if you have any other ideas."

"You really like him. I've never seen you shy away from having some awkward conversation like this before."

"Just help me okay?"

She nods, her face turning serious. "Just, initiate it. The next time y'all are snuggling or whatever. Make a move, Maura. Lord knows you're not shy."

I grimace. My past few months of one-night stands flash before my eyes.

"I didn't mean it like that. I meant that you're comfortable with who you are, confident. So be yourself and guide him along and if he's uncomfortable, he'll pull back or try to talk to you about it, and then you guys can go from there. But I highly, highly doubt he'll pull back."

"That makes sense." I agree slowly. "God, I hope I make the right move."

"You need to have sex."

"I need to have earth-shattering sex."

"Preach."

OPERATION: *Seduce Zack Huntington.*

When he enters my dorm just before 10PM, I'm ready for him.

Clad in a pair of boy shorts and a shirt that barely covers my ass, I'm leaning against my headboard, a textbook propped on my bent legs, skimming the reading for class tomorrow.

"Hey," Zack bends to place a kiss on my cheek. "How was your day?" His eyes scan my legs, a smile ghosting his lips as his gaze lingers on the toe ring on my left foot.

"Pretty good. I submit two of my final papers this week. And my Photography final is coming along, nearly done. You?"

"I'm curious to see your final project." He sits on my bed, taking my feet and placing them in his lap. "My day was okay. Better now that I'm here."

Closing my book with a thud, I drop it to the floor next to my bed. I pull my legs out of his lap and shift so that I'm kneeling beside him. "Do you have any studying to do?"

"Nope, I'm all yours."

Make a move, Maura.

It's ridiculous, really, that in this moment with a guy I've shared more secrets with than anyone in the past few months, I'm nervous. I never felt nervous with Hector or any of the randoms, but with Zack everything's different. He's the one who makes me feel like myself again, like I'm whole.

He's the one who has the ability to rip me to pieces all over again.

My palms feel sweaty and my heart thuds loudly in my chest. I study his face for any type of hesitancy, but he just glances at me expectantly.

I can do this.

I'm brave as fuck.

"Good," I say finally, and my voice is low and husky with a hint of my nerves skirting around the edges. Placing my hands on the tops of his shoulders, I swing my right knee across his lap so I'm straddling him. Winding my left hand behind his neck, I shift my weight so I'm lined up with him perfectly. I grin at his surprised expression, the widening of his eyes, the sharp intake of breath.

Undeterred , I lower my mouth to his and kiss him. Slowly, carefully, reverently.

And it takes exactly three seconds for all of Zack's restraint to snap.

Mission accomplished.

45

ZACK

J esus.

Maura's kiss surprises the hell out of me.

But the instant my mind registers that she's straddling me, leaning into me with soft touches, my body reacts and the careful consideration I've been treating her with morphs into a fire of need. I've been trying for weeks to hold back, but now that she's made the first move, all bets are off.

I'm ready to show her that I crave her more than my next breath.

Flipping her beneath me, her back hits the center of the mattress as I hover above her on my hands and knees, staring down at her wild eyes and swollen lips.

"Jesus, you're the most beautiful woman I've ever seen. After tonight, you're one-hundred percent mine, baby."

Her fingers come up slowly, tugging on the collar of my hoodie, as she pulls me closer. And that's all the encouragement I need to dip my lips down to her waiting mouth, cover her body with my own. I kiss her hard, loving when her lips part beneath mine, giving me access to her mouth.

My tongue darts in, dancing with hers, as my left hand

grips her hip. Her palms slide up my ribcage, pulling my T-shirt and hoodie up as she goes. When she gets to my shoulders, I push up onto my knees to tug both over my head before collapsing back over her frame.

Her fingers explore my bare chest, rolling over my abdomen, as I capture her mouth again. The touch of her lips against mine lights me up like fire and I want to consume her until we both burn out.

Rolling onto my side, I pull her body toward mine. Cradling her face, she presses her cheek against my fingers, as my left-hand slides over her bare thigh, my fingers playing with the bottom of her boy shorts.

When Maura bites her lip, I continue my exploration. Gliding my hand over her hip, I work my way under her shirt until I reach the swell of her breast. She moans as I palm her, working her nipple between my thumb and index finger.

And that sound is the last thing I hear as we crash into each other at a frenzied pace. The sweet and slow ignites into hard and desperate. Her fingers make short work of the buttons on my jeans. I roll her over me so she's straddling me once more and pull her shirt off in one swift movement.

She leans down to kiss me, and I let her have the upper hand for several moments before flipping her beneath once more. Her legs fall open as my knee nudges between them. She tugs my jeans lower. I shimmy her boy shorts down her hips, past her thighs and over her knees, until they pool near her feet. My boxers disappear next.

Hovering over her, her eyes widen, vulnerability mixed with desire. Her teeth rake over her bottom lip and I inhale, drinking her in. Dropping my mouth to her neck, I work my way down her body, covering every inch of her skin with my kiss, my touch.

I work her over until she's writhing beneath me, her nails digging into my shoulders, scoring my back. "Please Zack."

"You sure about this, baby?"

"Yes. I want this. I want this with you."

Those are the only words I need to hear before capturing her lips once more and we tangle together in hot moments of exploration, desperation, and urgency.

———

MAURA and I fall back to reality tangled in each other's sweaty embraces, our breathing deep and labored. Soft curls stick to her forehead and the back of her neck. My hand ghosts over the dip of her hip before settling on the smooth skin of her stomach. I pull her back into my chest and kiss the back of her neck. She sighs and we both sink into the pillows lining her headboard.

"That was …" She trails off.

I run my nose down the curve of her neck, resting my forehead against the top of her shoulder where I press another kiss.

"Amazing." She's breathless, her voice a mixture of awe and relief and giddiness.

"You're amazing, Maura."

She turns in my arms so her hands are curled up against my chest. "I didn't think … I didn't know it could be like that," she admits, a faint blush working its way up her neck.

"Like what?"

"Like, more than just physical. That was more than anything I've ever experienced. Deeper. The connection. It was just…more. Meaningful, I guess. Am I making sense?"

I chuckle, brushing a kiss over her mouth. God, I can't keep my hands off her. Or my lips. "It makes perfect sense.

And," I hold her chin with my finger to make sure she sees the truth in my eyes, "I felt it too."

I don't want to give her any more space, any more time to figure things out. This changed everything. I want her to be mine, and I want to be hers and that's the end of it. From here on out we should tackle everything, all of the hurdles she's trying to get past and all of the challenges that come up, together. As a couple.

"Maura." I dip my head to catch her gaze.

"Hmm?" She looks up sleepily, her eyes glazed with the dreamy afterglow of phenomenal sex and the pull of sleep.

"Be with me."

"I am with you."

"Be with me for real. Be my girlfriend."

She nods, lifting her mouth for another kiss. "Yes."

46

MAURA

"I have a boyfriend."

"What?" Lila exclaims.

"Hell yeah!" Emma hollers. "Oh, Zack Huntington, be still my beating heart."

"Nice work, Maura!" Mia grins.

"Tell us everything. Leave out no details." Lila demands.

Smiling at their surprised faces in Google Hangout, I spill the details.

"Wow, it's almost like Adrian sent Zack to you, isn't it?" Mia wonders aloud.

"You know, I haven't thought of it like that but yeah, it does feel that way sometimes." I guess Adrian is still looking out for me.

"How do you feel about it all?" Lila asks.

"I feel really great. Like I'm growing back into myself, the Maura I was before. Just, with a superhot boyfriend."

"Super hot." Emma echoes.

"I can't wait for you all to spend time with him."

"At every single one of your spring regattas?" Mia grins.

"Exactly."

"I'm so happy for you, Maura!" Lila leans closer to the screen. "You look so happy."

"I am." I say. And it's the truth.

INHALE, exhale, clear your mind. You're going to be fine.

The words run through my head like a mantra but when I look out into the sea of faces comprising my Photography class, I feel anything but fine.

I feel nauseous, dizzy, and ill.

Don't pass out.

Clad in black boots, black tights, a gray mini, and a white button-down shirt, I look the part for my presentation. But I don't feel the confidence required to speak about my assignment, my emotions, the world I see through my lens in front of nearly twenty people.

"Maura." Professor Minela smiles. "Whenever you're ready."

Deep breath. Inhale, exhale, clear your mind.

You're going to be fine.

"Good morning," I begin, my voice shaking slightly. "My name is Maura Rodriguez and I'm a senior at McShain University. I'm a member of the women's rowing team and have been since I started at McShain. Some of you may have heard of me, particularly after my twin brother, Adrian died last May. When I first chose my topic for this assignment, I was pissed."

A couple titters sound around the room before silence ensues again.

"I thought my topic was unfair, given my situation, given the grief I was dealing with."

Several students sit up straighter, lean forward in their

seats. I have their attention. All of them. And for some reason, instead of making me shake in panic, their focus on my presentation is calming.

This is a story I can tell. This is my truth. And I'm tired of hiding from it.

"But really, I was just afraid. Scared that if I started to delve into my topic, everyone would be able to see that I've become it." I smile wryly. "Because my topic is broken. And that's the only way to describe how I've felt since Adrian died."

I turn to my first photograph, placed on a stand in front of the entire room. There are four of them, all lined up, telling the story of my healing. Removing the white boards in front of each photograph, I place them in the corner as a gasp trickles through the crowd.

My final project, my truth, my freaking heart, is on full display.

Swallowing the emotions in my throat, I turn back to the room and walk to stand next to the first photo.

A variety of different-colored, various-shaped pills, crushed and broken and crumbled, fills the photo. Scattered throughout the pills is several prescription vials, empty among the dying grass of early winter. "I was inspired to create and take this photo because this is how I became broken. My brother overdosed on prescription painkillers that were laced with fentanyl. He had been taking pills without the knowledge of a doctor for weeks to self-medicate an old back injury in order to row. Hiding his addiction from his family, his friends, his teammates, I imagine he thought he had everything under control. I don't think he ever realized how fragmented his decision would leave us all. I don't think he ever considered that a bunch of broken pills could end his life."

I fist my fingers in my skirt for a moment, collecting myself as I walk to my second photograph. It's a photo of broken beer bottles, cut off at their necks, wine bottles smashing in midair, crushed vodka and tequila bottles thrown in on the black asphalt for good measure. The glass is shining on the pavement of the parking lot, the sunlight reflecting off the colors. "Trading one vice for another," I joke. "The second photograph for my final project is what I turned to in the wake of Adrian's death. Alcohol. Lots and lots of drinking. I thought consuming enough alcohol would make me forget, would help numb all the feelings rushing through me, all the anger that I couldn't process. I mistakenly thought that by going out and partying, I was moving on.

In reality, I was just giving myself permission to wallow in my brokenness, because drinking didn't fix anything. It just provided a pause, a break from my life. Eventually, it all came crashing down." I flash a tight smile at my class before discussing the technicality of the photo: the ridiculously fast exposure time necessary to capture the breaking wine bottles, the shutter release trigger I used with help from advanced equipment I had to borrow—and swear over and over not to break—from the Photography supervisor, additional soft boxes I used for lighting. This was a difficult photograph to capture and it took many attempts. Luckily, I had the extra empty wine bottles. Plus, the added glass already broken on the ground added to the image I was hoping to capture.

"And this brings me to my third photograph." I study the photo for a moment. It's difficult to make out what it is since it's such a close up. But if you take the time to study the picture, you can tell that it's the yarn of blankets, in the pale pastels that comprise a nursery. A soft pink, a light yellow, a muted blue, a sweet green. The yarn is knitted in different patterns and the colors blend together with bits of white running through them, separating them, joining them.

"I took this photo using the macro mode and no flash. I used the timer and a tripod to ensure no movement. This is a photograph of baby blankets, representing broken dreams." I gulp at the air then, trying to keep my tears checked. And while I'm not going to share with my class about the loss of my baby, it didn't feel right to overlook the role he or she played in my healing process. Because the truth is that my baby helped me find hope for the future again, my baby gave me a moment of clarity, a purpose, that spurred my healing journey. "When we are babies, our parents have all of these amazing dreams for us. For the people we will grow into, for the things we will accomplish, for the passions we will embrace. As we grow older, those dreams shift and change and develop. And sometimes, those dreams are cut short completely. But for that short amount of time that we are wrapped in the soft blankets of our childhood, anything seems possible, everything within reach. And nothing is really broken. Until we break it ourselves." Stepping forward, I clasp my hands in front of my waist. "Strangely, it was the loss of a dream, the loss of an expectation, that gave me the clarity and the strength to move forward. For me, this photograph represents loss just as much as it represents hope. And for me, this photo is meant to heal broken."

I exhale and approach my final photograph. It's a series of four oars slicing through the Schuylkill River, interrupting its smoothness, its calm, and creating a ripple. I explain the slow shutter speed and small aperture I used to capture the droplets of water dripping from the oars, falling back to the water. "This is a photograph I took of the LaFarge men's team practicing. My brother rowed for LaFarge. In the photo we can see the oars slicing through the water, breaking its flat surface, turning a smooth surface into a choppy, tumultuous one. I chose to take this photo for several reasons. After Adrian's death, after I broke, rowing seemed like both a curse and a salvation to me. It was a curse because it tied me to so many memories I had of my twin, some I was trying to forget. And it was a salvation because it tied me to so many memories I had of my twin, some I would give anything to remember in perfect clarity. Rowing was always the thing I turned to when I couldn't shut my mind off, it instills me a calmness that helps me process, helps me make sense of things. It was an important component in trying to mend some of the cracks I was struggling with. And lastly, I always loved that moment, the one at the start where all the boats are lined up. The sun is shining down on us and for an instant, everything is perfectly still. Sounds cease, the shells are in a perfectly straight line, and even the water stops moving. It's this complete calmness before utter chaos begins. A sort of calm before the storm. But the moment of crazy chaos that comes afterwards is amazing. And I've learned this semester, especially through this assignment, that sometimes broken is beautiful and that being broken, feeling pain and anguish and despair, can eventually make you whole. Thank you."

I stand still as the class drinks in my photographs for one more moment before applause breaks out. Professor Minela comes forward and wraps an arm around my shoulders as my classmates continue to clap before Q and A.

Releasing a shaky breath, I smile, relieved that my presentation is over, pleased with the overall outcome of my final project, and feeling some of my jagged, broken pieces snap back together.

47

ZACK

I t's strange, that moment when you walk into a home you've been in a thousand times, sometimes treated like your own, and everything is suddenly different.

Or maybe you're just different.

Whatever the reason, that's how it feels when I walk into the Rodriguez home at Maura's side.

It's as if the million memories of me sitting at the dinner table as Adrian's friend, sleeping over and helping myself to coffee in the morning, spending holidays with the family, never really happened. Because now I'm not here as Adrian's best friend but as Maura's boyfriend. And everything feels different even though the house is exactly the same.

I was surprised when Maura asked me to have dinner with her and her parents. I know she really pulled away from them after Adrian passed. She barely brought them up in conversations and when she did, it was with a grimace. But I guess part of the healing process, part of moving forward, is making amends. And so here we are, standing in the foyer of the Rodriguez family home.

Mr. Rodriguez shakes my hand, his eyes curious as to

why I'm here with Maura. Mrs. Rodriguez seems elated to see me, pulling me into a hug that feels motherly and familiar. "I'm so happy you guys are here for dinner. I was so surprised when Maura called to tell me she was coming over tonight. And bringing you with her!" she gushes, guiding us into the living room. "How are finals, Maura?" And before Maura can answer, "How are you Zackary? It's so good to see you again."

Maura tugs me down next to her on the couch. "Finals are great, Mom. And I wanted to come home for dinner tonight to see you guys and to introduce you and Dad to my boyfriend." She drops the news like a bombshell, and I bite the inside of my mouth to keep from smiling.

Way to go, Maura! No lead-up there. Poor Mr. and Mrs. Rodriguez.

I watch for their reactions as I keep Maura's hand tucked in mine.

Mrs. Rodriguez's face lights up, "Oh my God! You and Zack?" she exclaims, her hand covering her mouth as her eyes dart between Maura and me. "Why, that's the best news I've heard in ages!"

"Thanks, Mrs. R."

We all look to Mr. R. He's quiet, eyeing me speculatively. Removing myself from Mrs. R's embrace, she grips my arm and turns toward her husband. "Henry?"

He shakes his head, a small smile appearing on his face. "I'm just surprised is all," he clarifies. "You sure about him, mi melon de corazon?"

"Yes, Dad."

"Well then," He walks toward me and I meet him half-way. He throws an arm around my shoulder. "You always were part of this family, son. It's good to have you back at the dinner table."

"It's good to be back, sir. And thank you."

Drinking wine and filling my plate with roasted pork, plantains, and rice, we talk about rowing, about politics, about mine and Maura's plans after graduation.

And a strange déjà vu feeling settles over me as I laugh and talk and look over at Maura.

In many ways, it's like I've returned home.

AT NIGHT, Maura and I sit in our usual picnic spot on her bedroom floor and eat the coconut pudding that Mrs. R sent home with us.

"This is delicious." I heap another spoonful into my mouth.

"Mom was really happy you came for dinner. Before I even told her that we were together. I think she misses you."

"It was really nice to see your parents again. And to eat Mama R's home cooking."

"Yeah. But it was weird, right? Like everything felt totally normal even though it's all different?"

"Yes. I kept thinking the same thing. It was almost like déjà vu. I kept expecting Adrian to walk down the stairs."

"I know." She eats a bite of pudding and takes a sip from the coffee she's drinking. "You know, I'd like to meet your family."

"Really?" I ask, surprised. "They're all certifiably crazy. Especially my sister."

Maura snorts. "I don't care. I'd like to meet them anyway. I feel like you know so much about me, about my family. Hell, you're already an honorary Rodriguez. I've got some catching up to do."

I mull over her words, touched that she would want to

make a trip all the way to Nebraska. "You know you'll have to come to a square state for that to happen, right?"

"As long as I don't have to go cow tipping or whatever you people do for fun."

"Don't worry. We'll just make you party in a barn, ride ATVs, and shoot a gun."

Her eyes widen, a streak of panic crossing her face.

"I'm kidding," I snicker at her reaction. "You're going to be disappointed when you realize my family lives in a subdivision that could sit in any suburban town in the country. Can you come for New Years? Unless you have plans with your friends."

"Really? I mean, I don't have any plans. But would that be okay? Is it too soon? Do you think they'll like me?"

Chuckling, I reach out a hand out to quiet her stream of questions.

Who would have thought that steel nerves Maura would be nervous about meeting the Huntington clan? "It's more than okay. My mom will be over the moon, trust me. She'll probably make you go to a holiday-themed flea market with her and Pinterest a craft. I promise, everyone will love you. And it's definitely not too soon."

"Then let's celebrate New Year's Eve together." She licks pudding off her bottom lip. "And, after New Year's, do you want to come to New York with me?"

"What's in New York?"

She scrapes her spoon against the plate, scooping up extra pudding. "Cade planned a reunion for Lila. Well, it's kind of for all of us. It's January 7 in New York. I want you to meet my friends for real, not just in passing at some crew party, but as my boyfriend. Will you come?"

"As if that's even a question."

Maura beams. "Good."

"ARE you bringing anyone special home for Christmas this year, Zackary?" Mom's eyes light up as I FaceTime with my family.

They're decorating the ridiculously oversized Christmas tree in our living room. Behind the tree, I can make out the candles flickering in the big bay window at the front of our house. Off to the side, mistletoe hangs from the doorway leading to the kitchen. The entire room is washed in reds and greens and golds. I snort as Nicole dances behind Mom, her eyes wide with curiosity and Dad rolls his eyes, turning to place a macaroni ornament I made in third grade on the tree.

I shake my head and Mom's face falls.

"No, Mom, not for Christmas. For New Year's though," I laugh as her face lights back up.

"Really?"

"Really."

"Oh, Zack!" Mom's hand flies up to cover her heart. "That's lovely, really. Is this Adrian's sister, Maura?"

I try to cut Nicole a look over Mom's shoulder, but my sister turns and suddenly becomes interested in the ornaments dangling from the tree.

"Yeah, Mom."

"Oh, I can't wait to meet her. Don't worry, we won't scare her off."

Nicole turns at this and flashes me an evil grin, tapping her fingertips together behind Mom's back.

Dad snorts and does a weird dance in the background.

Yeah right. My family is going to go to great lengths to embarrass the hell out of me.

"Sure," I say.

"I'll start preparing the guest room."

"Mom, it's weeks from now."

"Oh, Zackary." She waves a hand at me. "It has to be perfect."

Just getting to kiss Maura at midnight on New Year's Eve is all the perfect I need.

LEAVING the Architecture building after my last final, I pull my hoodie up.

It's bitterly cold out but the bite in the air does little to dampen my spirits. I'm done with finals and tomorrow, Maura and I board a flight to Boston.

"Zack! Zack, wait up."

I turn to see who's calling my name and nearly collide with Lauren. My hands shoot out to steady her before she falls.

"Hey."

"Hi."

Narrowing my eyes, I wait her out, suspicious as hell.

"I just wanted to say I'm sorry."

"For telling Maura that I killed her brother? For pretending you were pregnant? For lying?"

"For all of it. I was wrong for the way I treated you this semester. I just … I love you, Zack." She looks up at me then and her eyes are sincere. "I always thought we'd end up together, you know?"

"Lauren."

"I know how I handled everything was wrong. It was desperate. And I shouldn't have tried to manipulate you or threaten your future with Maura. I was jealous." She shrugs. "Anyway, I just wanted to tell you that I'm sorry. And Merry Christmas." She smiles, her fingers going up to touch the pendant on her necklace. Two interlocking hearts. Once mine and hers.

I groan inwardly. It's hard to just erase someone from your life because they messed up. A bunch of good moments, happy memories that Lauren and I shared flash through my mind. And really, now that Maura and I are together, I'm not even that upset by her past actions, her behavior. Because now Lauren doesn't really mean much more to me than a sweet romance I had in college.

Maura, she's my future.

"Merry Christmas, Lauren."

With that closure in place, I head home to pack for Boston.

48

MAURA

"**N**ervous?" Zack smirks, lacing our fingers together as we descend over Boston Harbor.

"I'm not much of a flier."

He chuckles, glancing at my white knuckles locked in his hand. "No kidding?"

"Shut up." I squeeze his hand but the laugh that falls from my lips eases the tension in my neck and shoulders. "We never flew much growing up. Before going to McShain, I'd only ever been on a plane when we would visit Puerto Rico every few summers."

"Yeah, we didn't fly a ton growing up either. Not until Nicole and I got older. Then all of a sudden Mom got this travel bug and insisted we see the country as a family." He chuckles. "We would take these random trips to places like Minnesota and Idaho while everyone else was going skiing in Aspen or to New York."

The plane touches ground with a bounce before we roll down the runway.

"Welcome to Logan International Airport." The flight attendant's voice announces over the intercom.

"We're here." Zack squeezes my hand before unlacing his fingers. "Hopefully the weather holds. I've got a lot planned for us."

"Really?"

"Really." He leans forward and presses a kiss against my lips before scooting around me to reach into the overhead bin and grab our carry-on bags. "Welcome to Boston."

The cab ride to our hotel, situated in the heart of Copley Square, is quick. Along the way, I can't stop staring out the window as we pass new structures, old, brick buildings, and Fenway Park. Adrian would have loved to see the historic baseball field. He would have clamored for us to do a tour and would have posed for photos in front of the banners announcing all of the Red Sox World Series wins.

Our hotel is in a perfect location, walking distance to all the major attractions. When we enter our hotel room, Zack drops our bags on the floor and digs through his suitcase for winter boots and extra socks.

Looking around the room, my eyes zero in on the king-sized bed. Suddenly, I feel nervous, shy.

I'm on a getaway with a boy.

And not just any boy, but my boyfriend.

A guy I'm falling in love with.

A man I want to build a future with.

And here we are, sharing a hotel room, sharing a bed, like a couple who has been together forever. Comfortable in each other's presence, relaxing into the silences that stretch between us, sharing our darkest secrets, our deepest fears.

Perching on the edge of the bed, Zack comes toward me. He leans down, places his palms flat on either side of me, and presses a scorching kiss against my mouth.

I moan under his touch and he chuckles. Whenever he's near, it's like my body senses him, is tuned into him, and hums with a desire that borders on needy. Now that I've had him, he's all I can think about. Zack Huntington simultaneously consumes me and heals me.

"Come," he pulls back, extending his hand to me. "If we don't leave now, we'll spend the whole day in bed. Not that *that* would be a bad thing, but we've got a city to conquer and crab cakes to eat."

"Ah, my fake blue blood." I tease, wrapping a heavy scarf around my neck.

When we're both bundled, only our eyes, noses, and mouths visible, we take the elevators to the ground floor and step out into the freezing, biting cold.

But on the inside, I'm burning up under Zack's glance, his touch, even his proximity.

49

ZACK

G oing to Boston in December is just plain stupid.
But I don't care.

Because one of the best moments of my life happens while we're standing in line at Mike's Pastry.

"You need to eat a cannoli." I tell Maura as she shifts her weight from foot to foot.

"Are you sure this is necessary? It's really cold."

"I'm positive. It's a rite of passage."

"To what?"

"Embracing Boston."

"You're lucky I love you; you know that?"

I bite the inside of my cheek, staring at her, etching each detail of her face into my memory. The surprise and seriousness of her stare, the way she keeps working her lower lip between her teeth, how her head tilts to the left as she waits for me to say something.

"Say it again." I squeeze the hand she has tucked into my Canada Goose jacket.

Maura rolls her eyes, huffing. "I love you, Zack Huntington."

Grinning, I dip my head and kiss her. "I love you more, Rodriguez."

She smiles, her face brightening, and my chest constricts at how beautiful she is. Rocking toward me, she stands on her toes as I cup the side of her face. Then, her lips collide with mine and the line, Mike's Pastry, hell, Boston, disappears.

A few whistles ring out from the waiting customers standing in line with us, and we pull back, laughing.

"You're crazy," I tell her.

"You're weird."

And I kiss her again, never able to get enough.

At the front of the line, we order cannoli and cappuccinos and carry our pastries to Faneuil Hall marketplace. Sitting on a bench in the middle of the town square, we huddle together, shivering, as we eat cannoli and immerse ourselves in the warmth of each other's kisses.

And it is perfect.

This moment and all the moments leading up to now *are* our reality. Falling in love is like that. It's everything at once and even though most of the time you can't tell which way is up, it's so good that you don't want to. It's sweet and crazy and challenging and hilarious. It sneaks up on you and suddenly you don't want to pass another day without that person by your side. Some people, they can pinpoint the exact moment they fell in love. Others don't know exactly when it happened, just that once it did, they never wanted to lose it.

For me, I started falling for Maura the day we went mini-golfing. I didn't admit it at the time, but since that morning when she walked to my SUV and lifted her fingers in a wave, I was hooked. Secretly, I think I knew she was for me the whole time, always meant to be mine.

I think I knew it all the while.

50

MAURA

Telling Zack I love him is one of the scariest, most exhilarating, best moments of my life.

I can't believe the words pop out of my mouth until they do, but I don't care. Because it's the truth.

I love him.

I'm in love with him.

And that feeling, taking that giant leap into a gallant freefall, is too sweet not to cherish.

We walk around the city for hours after consuming an absurd amount of calories from Mike's Pastry. Zack shows me Paul Revere's house, the *Cheers* pub, the cemetery that holds Sam Adams. We meander around the MIT and Harvard campuses, duck into random coffee shops for hot chocolate refills, and spend hours in the Boston aquarium. Walking up Newbury Street, we window shop and randomly buy winter gear like extra scarves and hats and gloves to keep us warm from the freezing cold.

We act like tourists, giddy and excited and joking about nothing. Or maybe we act like college kids in love for the first time. Either way, my cheeks ache from smiling and my heart feels lighter than it has in a long, long time.

At night, after a delicious meal of clam chowder and Zack's prized crab cakes, we snuggle beneath the covers of our king-sized bed. I press my cold toes against the warm skin of Zack's legs, and he laughs, drawing me into his arms. We lose ourselves in each other's touches and kisses until the early morning light draws shadows on the walls.

Lying there, with my head sharing Zack's pillow, listening to the quiet rhythm of his breath, I allow myself to revel in the certainty of a future I ignored for too long.

Now, my future is intertwined with Zack's.

And *that*, that makes all the difference.

51

ZACK

"Jingle bell, jingle bell, jingle bell rock!" Dad's voice rings out, singing along with the radio, as he passes out the Christmas presents scattered under the tree.

Nicole rolls her eyes, taking the box from his hands. "Another one for me!" She sticks her tongue out in my direction, placing the present in her pile of gifts.

"Sorry, dear, that one's for Maura," Mom says gently, removing the gift from Nicole's pile and adding it back to the presents nestled next to the manger.

I snicker at Nicole's expression, and she reaches over to punch me in the arm.

"I swear you two still act the same as you did when you were eight and nine-years-old on Christmas morning." Mom attempts to scold us but her face beams with delight. These are the moments she lives for, and who are Nicole and I to get in the way of that?

"Thanks, Dad." I take the gift he offers me, noting the expertly tucked and taped wrapping. "Mom really needs to be a grandmother so you better get on it," I whisper to Nicole, holding up one of the boxes that is covered in ribbons and bows.

"You may beat me to that."

I'm not even going to touch that comment.

"When is Maura flying in, Zackary?" Mom asks.

"On the morning of the thirty-first."

"Should we all go pick her up from the airport?"

"That's a great idea!" Nicole claps her hands together.

"That's okay," I say quickly, looking to Dad for help.

"Meg, let the boy have a moment to greet his girl in private," Dad says, putting an arm around Mom to soften the blow. "We all know you'll get your hands on her the second she walks through the door, and Zack may have to fight you off to get his kiss at midnight."

Nicole cracks up.

Mom blushes.

"Thanks for your help, Dad," I say dryly.

"Anytime," He answers, my sarcasm going over his head. "Now, the presents have been passed out."

"Not counting the gifts from Santa that are at Nana and Pop's house," Mom adds.

Oh my God. She's serious.

"You're right," Nicole whispers. "We need to start growing this family. Or convince Cam to start sleeping here on Christmas Eve."

"Let's open the gifts!" Mom beams.

I tear into the paper of my first present just like the eight-year-old Mom mentioned.

Christmas morning in my house has always been a series of traditions. Family rituals. Nicole and I waking early to find the overwhelming number of presents resting underneath the Christmas tree, the fireplace already lit and crackling,

Christmas music playing from the speakers. We always drink hot chocolate with lots of marshmallows and whipped cream and eat bacon and eggs for breakfast. We argue with Mom about attending church, but somehow always end up in the first pew. Our tree is always decorated in silver and gold, with an angel perched at the top. Every few years, Dad pulls out the train set from his childhood and sets it up to run circles around the tree. Candles light each and every window, and Mom changes out the throw pillows on the couch to reflect the Christmas spirit.

And even though it seems ridiculous and childish and incredibly traditional, all of us Huntingtons sitting beneath the Christmas tree in our pajamas, Dad passing out gifts, Mom snapping photos on her camera, I can't help but love it. It's a comforting reminder of my childhood, a familiar throwback to simpler times and happy occasions.

Watching my family now, as Dad slaps a bow in Nicole's hair and Mom kisses Dad adoringly on the cheek, I can't help but aspire for this one day. With my own family. With Maura. Sure, I still want to go to graduate school, to live in Manhattan, to secure an awesome job with a big firm; I'm not in a rush or anything.

But eventually, one day, I want this.

With Maura drinking hot chocolate next to me.

52

MAURA

"Welcome aboard." The flight attendant greets me as I enter the airplane.

"Thanks." I fist my boarding pass as I make my way down the aisle and locate my seat. Ten A. Stowing my carry-on bag in the overhead bin, I slide into the seat, plug my headphones in, and select a playlist on Spotify.

I'm flying to Omaha, Nebraska.

I almost laugh to myself. I never anticipated I would ever travel to the Midwest, but here I am having my second adventure in nearly as many weeks.

The plane is nearly empty, not surprising since Omaha doesn't strike me as a party place to ring in the new year. Still, I'm excited to see Zack, to stand next to him for the countdown, to kiss him at midnight.

And, to give him his Christmas gift: a five-day getaway to Playa del Carmen, Mexico before we're required to be back on our campuses for crew. Mom and Dad bought our flights as their Christmas gift to us. I know he's going to be surprised, and I can't wait to see the look on his face when he opens the present.

Staring out the window, the plane gathers speed, barreling down the runway and lifting into the air. Below, the houses grow smaller, the cars resemble ants, and people disappear completely.

Closing my eyes, I reflect on the past four months.

The College Pact.

Literally running into Zack.

The series of poor decisions and late nights out that resulted in my little wonder.

The grief and loneliness that finally eased with Zack's support.

My journey. One of healing. Of acceptance. Of forgiveness.

Of love.

Even though I couldn't have known any of this while it was occurring, I'm relieved that my dark and often desperate path led me to now. I'm thankful that my experiences this semester made me stronger, more empathetic.

But I'm most grateful for Zack.

Sometimes like a shadow, sometimes like a conscience, sometimes like my counterpoint, he was always there.

All the while.

MAY

53

MAURA

Our boat is completely still, everyone poised in position, as we wait in anticipation for the start. I pull the brim of Adrian's Toronto Blue Jays hat lower over my eyes to block the glaring sun. Behind me, Amber shifts in her seat.

This is it.

The women's Varsity Eight finals. Six boats, all racing to be the number one team in the United States. And it has to be us. It has to be.

"Settle down now," our coxswain, Amanda, says, her fingertips tapping the outside of the boat. "Here we go."

We steady ourselves in the start position and when the horn blares, we are perfectly in sync as we slide back to a half stroke. The race is underway in seconds, water splashing, our bodies bending in unison, Amanda's instructions floating on top of the breeze.

The wind beats against my skin and whistles in my ears.

Loud screams and cheers from spectators ring out, but I don't turn my head, don't do anything to jeopardize the concentration of the boat, the focus we are all giving to this singular moment.

I know somewhere out there, Lila, Emma, and Mia are lined up, waving our school colors and homemade posters.

I'm sure Zack is leaning over the railing of his boathouse, my parents flanking him, staring right at me as our boat moves closer to the finish line.

And I know, from the bottom of my heart, that Adrian is watching over me, cheering me on, and encouraging me to dig in with everything I have.

"Keep it up! Six seat, slow your slide," Amanda's voice calls out. "Third five-hundred, turn it up!" She yells as we enter the third portion of the two thousand-meter race.

We push harder, lean deeper into our catches, keep our heels planted.

And then, we fly.

Our shell barely skims the top of the river as we fall into a rhythm so harmonious, so synchronized that everything else fades away.

It's just the nine of us in the boat, the purpose of this race, the significance of this moment.

And we row.

"We're in first! Keep the lead. Hold the lead!" Amanda's voice is a mixture of elation and nerves.

We never break our pace, never second-guess our victory of this regatta. Moments later, we cross the finish line first. The cheers go up from the grand stands, but we're all too tired, too dazed, too overwhelmed to do anything for several seconds but sit and stare in shock.

"Maura!" Zack's voice calls out from the bank of the river. I look up and see him standing in his singlet and a pair of gym shorts, his hands cupping around his mouth so his voice carries. "You did it!"

I did it.

"Oh my God! We did it," I whisper.

We won the Dad Vail Regatta.

And that's when the pandemonium erupts. The girls scream, hugging and wiping errant tears from their faces. I clasp the brim of Adrian's hat, pressing my fingertips together hard, as if I'm pressing this moment, this memory, into him. And in a way I am. Because this race, the grueling hours of practice, the early mornings on the water, they were always for him.

We row to the dock slowly and climb out of the shell, half of the oars clanging down noisily on the wooden dock, the other half skimming the water. Glancing up, Zack pulls me into a hug, his lips hard against mine.

Over his shoulder, Mom and Dad embrace, silent tears welling in my mother's eyes.

"Holy guacamole! That was crazy!" Emma tugs me from Zack's embrace into her own.

"You were amazing!" Mia gushes, squeezing my hand.

"The best!" Lila echoes.

I take in this moment, the smiling faces of the people I love best, the warmth of my teammates' arms as they rest around my shoulders for a group photo, the cold tickle of champagne as it sprays down on us from the champagne shower some of the underclassmen shake up.

I breathe it all in and know that Adrian would be—is incredibly proud.

And I know that when Zack lines up at the start in another thirty minutes, Adrian will watch over his teammates, his old boat, as they take first place. He'll cheer at us later tonight as we party away one of our last evenings as college seniors, all of us riding the natural high of the day, of the victory.

And he'll continue to watch over us as we move forward in our lives, our days melting into years.

Even though he's not here, he'll always be with me, with us.

Of this, I am certain.

SEVEN YEARS LATER

EPILOGUE

Zack

"I'm dying. I'm dying!" Maura screams, pain filling the lines in her face, her eyes wide with fear. "No one told me it was going to be like this. Liars! You all lie!"

"You got this, baby. You're doing amazing." I brush sweaty curls away from her forehead. "Only a little longer now."

"You've been saying that for hours!"

"And you're getting closer."

"Twins! I can't believe we're having twins." She moans, closing her eyes and turning her head away from me as another contraction hits.

My hand is throbbing from Maura's squeezing, but I don't dare let go. We're approaching the fourteenth hour of labor and my girl is killing it.

"Almost there, baby."

"Okay, Maura. On the next contraction, you can push." Dr. Robbins instructs. "Dad, do you want to watch your babies come into the world?" He lifts the sheet covering Maura from the waist down.

"No fucking way!" Maura lurches up in bed, her eyes swinging to mine. "No way, Zack. I'm too young to kill our sex life."

Snickering, I nod, kissing her forehead. "I'll stay right here."

"Get ready to push." Dr. Robbins says as Maura's scream rips from her lungs.

Several pushes later, a new cry pierces the air.

My heart swells into my throat.

"It's a boy!" Dr. Robbins announces, passing the baby to a waiting nurse. "You're not done yet, Maura. A few more pushes." He instructs as Maura's face transforms to one of determination.

"Come on, Rodriguez."

Her face twists as another contraction moves through her body.

"Jesus." She wheezes out, her head slamming back into the hospital bed as the most beautiful sound in the world rings out.

"It's a girl!"

"Oh my God. A boy and a girl." Maura's eyes tear, pure happiness radiating from her face.

"You're so beautiful." I squeeze her hand as our babies are placed on her chest. "Oh wow, they're so little."

"They're perfect." She smiles down at two perfectly-round heads covered in a mass of curls. "I'm already in love."

Sitting on the edge of her bed, I run my finger along my little girl's cheek, awe and wonder filling me up. Her small mouth sucks and she cries out, feisty like her mama. "Hi, little babe."

My little guy squirms and looks up at me and my breath catches. "Hi buddy."

We stare at our little miracles in awe, watching as they squirm on Maura's chest, listening for every sound that falls from their mouths.

"Names?" I whisper.

"Adrian for the boy."

"Definitely. Just, hear out my girl name, okay?"

"Uh-oh. What is it?" Maura asks but her eyes spark.

"Our baby girl already has your spunk and Adrian's spirit."

"Name?" Maura asks skeptically.

"Adrianna."

Maura grins. "Adrian and Adrianna?"

"Adrian and Adrianna."

"They're perfect."

Wrapping my arms around my family, I say a silent prayer to my best friend for giving me the greatest treasures of my life.

THANK you so much for reading Zack and Maura's story! For some intrigue and suspense, dive into *Me + You*, Emma's delicious romance with a sexy, misguided boxer.

A SNEAK PEEK OF ME + YOU

Emma

"Toss another pancake this way, would ya?" I hold my plate out as Mia spears a pancake with the tines of her fork and holds it as far as humanly possible from her face. It plops down on my plate in a puddle of maple syrup. Delicious. "Girl, you're going to disappear one day if you only subsist on legumes."

Mia blushes as I pour a generous heap of syrup over my pancake. You can never have too much sweet maple goodness, am I right?

"Can you believe today is the day?" Lila squeals, a forkful of scrambled eggs hovering below her chin. "I mean, Mia, you're going to Rome!"

Maura rolls her eyes and coughs into her coffee mug.

Mia looks like she's about to vomit.

Reaching out a hand, I squeeze Mia's cold fingers. "Relax. You're going to be a rock star. This is good for you. For all of us."

"The college pact is everything." Lila adds, earning another eye roll from Maura.

"I love when you speak in superlatives." Maura quips.

Lila ignores her and ticks off the pact criteria on her fingers. "Push past our comfort zones, meet hot guys and date them, be brave and wild, have fun." Lila turns to me, pointing a finger accusingly. "And moving forward. No more being hung up on Josh McCannon."

"Gah! I'm not hung up on him."

Three sets of eyes stare at me, blinking.

"I'm not!"

"Em, Josh McCannon is an idiot. Any guy, any guy Em, would be lucky to date you. And no douchebag, especially not a stupid summer fling with a guy you went to high school with, should ever make you feel bad about yourself. I hate that he made you question your worth. The pact is about embracing everything we are." Lila rants.

Mia nods and even Maura tips her head in agreement.

Big sigh. Josh McCannon. A popular boy from high school whose path crossed with mine at a Memorial Day Weekend party in my home town. We drank too much, flirted a bit, exchanged a very sensual kiss... and continued to hook up for the rest of the summer. It was fun, and carefree, and simple in the way summer hookups are. Everything is of the moment, marking the present with more weight than it should hold in a "fling-type" scenario. It gives a girl ideas that maybe, just maybe, this summer fun could turn into an autumn reality.

And then, two weekends ago, *it* happened. Josh McCannon informed me, not politely either, that it was a fun thing, but he couldn't actually date me. For starters, I look nothing like his "type." Who knew he even had a type? Apparently, he does. His real girlfriend type is more along the lines of tall, blonde, and gorgeous. His real girlfriend type looks like Lila, which seems to be a theme in my life. However, my shorter, stockier build with a layer of chub around the middle and boring brown bangs is a definite hook-up only.

Alas, I digress.

Does it matter?

Probably not.

But after a series of put-downs from a series of guys I liked, the wind has gone out of my sails. I should definitely stop chasing guys that are out of my league. If I want to keep any of my confidence, that is.

"I know, I know." I tell my friends just so they'll stop talking about it. Him. The whole summer.

"I'm serious, Emma."

"So am I, Li."

"I'm going to miss you girls." Mia interjects, pushing her food around her plate.

Me too." I admit, a realization washing over our breakfast table. The four of us have been inseparable since we dormed together in a quad our freshman year at McShain University. We've been through every college milestone together: new relationships, breakups, drunken nights you wish would last forever, hungover mornings you wish you could die, changing majors, family illnesses, family drama, the gamut. But this semester, the start of our senior year, we're all being pulled in new directions for the first time. Ever.

Mia is boarding a plane to study abroad in Rome, Italy. Lila is heading to California to participate in a competitive medical internship program at Astor University. Maura is staying on campus, in Philadelphia, to prepare for her final season as a member of McShain's women's rowing team.

And me, well, I'm about to embark on a dream I've had

since the seventh grade. I'm interning on Capitol Hill in Washington, DC, for Senator LeBeau, from my home state, the Small Wonder of Delaware. Although now we're known more for our "Endless Discoveries." I'm still trying to sort that one out…

"Don't forget to update us with emails and FaceTime calls." Lila reminds Mia.

"Promise." Mia runs her fork over her untouched egg white omelet.

"In four months, we'll have the best stories to tell each other, the greatest experiences to share. Get pumped people." Lila raises her mimosa, her blue eyes dancing. "To the College Pact."

"To the College Pact," we echo, clinking our glasses and sharing a smile.

Champagne bubbles tickle my upper lip as I grin at my best friends. Josh McCannon who? This semester is going to be amazing.

Don't miss Emma and Luke's intense romance in *Me + You.*